THE GIRLFRIEND RESCUE

DISASTER CITY SEARCH AND RESCUE BOOK 1

JENNA BRANDT

COPYRIGHT

PRAISE FOR JENNA BRANDT

I am always excited when I see a new book by Jenna Brandt.

— Lori Dykes, Amazon Customer

Jenna Brandt is, in my estimation, the most gifted author of Christian fiction in this generation!

— Paula Rose Michelson, Fellow Author

Ms. Brandt writes from the heart and you can feel it in every page turned.

— Sandra Sewell White, Longtime Reader

For more information about Jenna Brandt visit her on any of her websites.

Signup for Jenna Brandt's Newsletter

Visit her on Social Media:

www.JennaBrandt.com
www.facebook.com/JennaBrandtAuthor
Jenna Brandt's Reader Group
hwww.twitter.com/JennaDBrandt
http://www.instagram.com/Jennnathewriter

THE GIRLFRIEND RESCUE

A search and rescue cop training to become a K-9 handler, a lovely dispatcher who always has his back, and an earthquake that threatens to tear them apart…

Officer Ted Hendricks has been biding his time, locating missing skiers and hikers for three years in Colorado, while waiting for a chance to become a K-9 handler. When a spot opens up at the Disaster City Search and Rescue facility in Texas, he jumps at the chance to go, even though it means leaving his girlfriend behind.

Dispatcher Deanna Harper had one strict rule — never date a cop. That all changed when she got to know Ted Hendricks. He was the only single officer in the department who didn't hit on her, which made him all the more appealing. When he decides to travel across the country to train as a K-9 handler, she decides he's worth taking a chance on a long distance relationship.

When Ted's team is deployed to help in the aftermath of an earthquake in Colorado, Ted finds out that Deanna was in the epicenter. Can Ted find Deanna in time to save her? Will Deanna be able to survive until he does? And if they reunite, will they find a way to be together despite the distance between them?

Step into the world of Disaster City Search and Rescue, where officers, firefighters, military, and medics, train and work alongside each other with the dogs they love, to do the most dangerous job of all — help lost and injured victims find their way home.

Dedicated to

my husband, Dustin, Badge #5654,

who inspired me to create this series.

You're not only my heart and soul,

but my own personal lawkeeper.

1

Ted Hendricks pulled his beanie cap down over his sandy blond hair to cover the edge of his ears. Even though spring was approaching, the Colorado mornings still held that crisp, cool air that made layers a necessity.

"You ready for your next search, Titan?" Ted asked his unofficial K9 partner, removing his leash and let him sniff the sock in his hand. "You've done great on the last two; let's make it three."

Titan sniffed several times, inhaling deeply. He turned and took off in the opposite direction. Ted followed, pleased that his partner was headed in the right direction. Every time he wondered if the K9 was going to underperform, Titan proved to Ted that he was the most capable search and rescue dog out there. It still shocked Ted that no one wanted to work with him after his police officer partner in Boulder was killed in a car accident. When the police bulletin went out to the county offering adoption for the dog, Ted immediately seized the opportunity. Not only was he a big animal person because he grew up on a farm just outside Clear Mountain, but he knew it was the perfect way to prove he could be a great additional K9 handler for the Clear Mountain Search and Rescue team.

Titan continued up the dirt trail, moving along the edge, stopping occasionally to take another whiff of whatever was driving him forward. About twenty yards further up the trail, Titan found the spot where the other matching sock had been hidden earlier in the day by Ted. He barked and sat down next to a bush on the side of the path.

Ted jogged up and dug inside the bush. He plucked out the sock with pride. "Great job, Titan, you did really good," he said, pulling out a treat from his cargo-pants' pocket and giving it to the German shepherd.

Titan barked a second time, wagging his tail with joy. Ted ruffled his partner's fur, laughing at how happy he was at his work. Ted had been worried whether or not they would bond and make a good team; however, the moment he picked him up from the Boulder County police kennel, there was an instant connection.

"You ready to head over and get Deanna?" Ted asked, as he re-attached the leash to Titan's collar.

He barked again, wagging his tail even faster at the mention of Ted's girlfriend. The only person Titan liked more than Ted was Deanna, and he couldn't blame his K9 friend. Deanna was amazing. Not only was she drop-dead gorgeous with curly red hair and bright green eyes, she was smart, funny, and one of the kindest people he knew. Even though he had worked with her for years, he had purposely never gone after her. He saw how it bothered her when the other men at the station hit on her, and he didn't want to be that guy. Plus, he didn't think he had time for a relationship when he was so focused on his career. When Deanna asked him out on a date, her pursuit was the first time he thought about the possibility of making room for anything other than his job and his family.

Once back at the parking lot of the Clear Mountain Resort, they loaded into Ted's truck and headed down the main road back into town. He drove to the east side of town and pulled up to a set of townhomes.

"Wait here, Titan. I'll be right back."

Ted hopped out of his truck and headed up the walkway. He reached the top of the steps and knocked on the door of the left unit. A few minutes later, Deanna opened the door. She was pulling on her last heel. "Just give me a quick sec," she said, moving over to grab her purse and jacket from the coat rack behind the door.

Ted grinned, repressing the chuckle that wanted to escape. It was so like Deanna to be late. She was as easy-going as they came in her personal life. This was probably her way of off-setting the need to be tough-as-nails when she was at work trying to keep up with the cops.

"Are we going to make it on time? I don't want your parents to be upset with me."

"We'll be fine," Ted promised, as he helped her into her black jacket. He hated covering up her blue blouse and jeans—which hugged the curves of her body perfectly—but he knew it was still a little too chilly to go anywhere without a coat. "Besides, they love you. You don't have anything to worry about."

"Good, because I know how important this is to your mom," Deanna said, locking the door behind her before they took off.

Saturday brunch was a tradition Ted's mother

started for the family when his first brother moved out on his own four years ago. As the youngest of the three brothers, Ted decided to move out two years ago. His mother complained all the time about having an empty nest now that they were all gone. It was probably why she liked Deanna so much. She thought it meant Ted would be settling down soon and giving her lots of grandchildren. His oldest brother, Phil, enjoyed the single life. Ken, the middle son, had only had one daughter from a previous relationship and swore he was done. This was the main reason their mother pinned all her hopes on Ted.

A few miles outside of town, they reached a dirt road that led to Ted's family's ranch. Set back and surrounded by trees was a rambling farmhouse with a wooden barn next to it. There were also two large silos and, next to the barn, a corral filled with horses.

Ted climbed out of the truck and came around to help Deanna climb down, then kept the door open to let Titan out as well. They made their way to the front of the house, but before they could even knock, the door swung open. "Uncle Teddy!" his six-year-old niece, Maggie, yelled with a giant grin on her face. "You ready to play Minecraft with me?" All of a sudden, noticing Titan, she pushed past Deanna and Ted to wrap her arms around the dog's neck. "Never mind, I want to play with Titan instead. Come on, boy," she said, gesturing for the K9 to follow her.

Ted and Deanna trailed after them into the dining room where the men were sitting around the table and his mother was putting out the last of the dishes.

"Can I help you with anything, Mrs. Hendricks?" Deanna offered.

"How many times do I need to remind you to call me Tamara?"

"I guess it's just a habit from my job. I tend to call everyone ma'am or by their last name," Deanna explained.

"Well, I suppose Mrs. Hendricks is better than ma'am. That would make me feel so old."

The men around the table chuckled.

"We wouldn't want that," Ken said, elbowing their brother Phil in the side. "Mom wants to pretend she's still twenty-two."

"Stop that," she chastised, patting her blonde mane. "Can I help it that I don't have a single gray hair on my head."

"Dying your hair will do that," Phil pointed out with a wry grin.

"I don't appreciate the accusation," she said, giving her son a withering look of anger. Turning her attention to Deanna, she added, "I don't need to dye. I have great genes. Just remember that, dear, when you and Teddy decide to finally get married and have children together. They're going to be blessed with the same great genes."

"Let's hurry up and eat before the game comes on. I want to find out who is going to make it to the state finals," Ted's father, Bill, said as he gestured to the empty seats next to him. "Sit down."

"Come on in here, Maggie," Ted's mother called out towards the living room. "It's time to eat."

Deanna and Ted did as they were directed just as Maggie came running into the room with Titan behind her. She took the last remaining chair at the table, and Titan laid down on the floor beside her.

His father said a prayer over the food before they passed the dishes of mashed potatoes, fried chicken, green beans, and bread around the table. The family laughed and talked about their week. Maggie kept slipping pieces of food to Titan. Ted knew he should probably stop it; it wasn't the best idea to feed him from the table, but he couldn't bring himself to stop it since it made them both so happy.

Just as they were finishing up the meal, Ted's cell phone buzzed. He picked it up and saw it was a call from work. "I have to take this." He answered the call only to be informed he was getting called in for a missing hiker. He wished he could take Titan with him and prove how great of a team they were, but he hadn't gotten up the nerve to seek the captain's approval yet. It would just have to wait until next time.

"Ken, do you mind giving Deanna a ride home for me?" Ted asked, standing up from the table. "I have to go to work. We've got a missing hiker."

"What about Titan?" Maggie asked, looking down at her K9 friend.

"Can you keep him here until I can pick him up later?" Ted asked.

"We can watch him, can't we, Daddy?" Maggie begged. "Please, Daddy, please?"

He shrugged. "Sure, I don't see why not."

Ted leaned over and gave Deanna a quick kiss. "Sorry about this. I'll call you later."

"I knew what I was signing up for when I

decided to date a search and rescue cop," she teased with a smile. "Go find that missing hiker."

As Ted took off, he was grateful for his wonderful family and girlfriend; however, part of him still longed for the one thing he didn't have that he always wanted. He wanted to be a K9 handler. He knew he needed to finally just go for it, but in the back of his mind, he worried that it wasn't going to work out. Pushing that troubling thought away, Ted focused on what he needed to do next. He sped towards the station, ready to meet his team, and start their search.

THE FIRST DAY back to work after Deanna Harper's weekend off was a doozy. Clear Mountain was a mid-size town, but you wouldn't know it from the number of calls in her queue at the moment. All morning, the phone had been ringing off the hook with calls for service directed to them from the county 9-1-1 center.

She worked her way through the calls one at a time, hoping to get done in time for her friend's arrival. Just as she was finishing up her final call,

Hayley Hall Bishop rushed into the room, seven months visibly pregnant.

"Let me guess, you're not going to have time for lunch?" Hayley asked as she came to rest at the edge of Deanna's desk.

Deanna held up one finger as she continued to speak into her microphone, "Copy that, Ocean Two, you are clear and can head to the next call pending. It's a burglary in progress, but be advised, it's Mrs. Mclintock. It's most likely cats in the alley." Deanna ended the call and leaned back in her chair, letting out a heavy sigh. "I thought today would be slow. Mondays usually are, but something must be in the water. It's been nonstop calls all day."

"I can go grab some lunch and bring it back here," Hayley offered, pushing her brown hair behind her ear.

"Would you mind? That sounds great. I didn't bring anything with me because I thought we would be going out to lunch. I don't know what I was thinking. I almost always end up eating lunch at my desk."

"You thought having a second dispatcher was going to make things easier for you, but I'm guessing that isn't the case."

Deanna shook her head. "I like Janet well

enough as a person, but I get the feeling she's here more for the socializing than the actual work." Deanna glanced around to make sure they were alone, then lowered her voice and added," I resent that the captain hired her without asking me first. I would have told him she had a reputation for being a badge bunny. On top of that, she's not professional at all. She's already late back from lunch—again—and with the amount of calls we've had today, I don't think I should leave her alone when she gets back."

"Believe me, I understand having to manage workers who don't take the job as seriously as you do. It's the story of my life at the Gazette."

"You have to deal with it way more than I do," Deanna pointed out. "I just have one problematic worker."

"Yes, but you've had to put up with the guys around here hitting on you, too. I can't even imagine having to deal with that day in and day out. I'd end up biting off someone's head if the men at the Gazette treated me the way the men around here treat you."

"I know from the outside it seems difficult, but the single men are usually on their best behavior in an effort to win me over. The guys who really bother me are the ones who think I got my job because of my looks. They act like there's nothing upstairs, and I'm just another badge bunny looking to land a cop for a boyfriend. It's why I was so resistant to dating cops to begin with. I didn't want to fall into that stereotype."

"You mean like Janet?" Hayley said with a roll of her eyes. "Isn't she on her fourth cop-boyfriend?"

"Fifth," Deanna corrected. "She dated three in Boulder before she moved to Clear Mountain."

"Well, at least everyone knows that you and Ted are the real deal. You passed up multiple chances to date plenty of guys around here."

Deanna nodded. "What can I say, the fact he didn't flirt with me, and never made me feel like a piece of meat was exactly why I was attracted to him. He didn't see me as a conquest, but as a real person with a brain and the ability to use it. It's the sexiest thing about him."

"Seriously? And the fact he's the most ripped guy at the station has nothing to do with it?"

"Hey now, I resent that comment," Connor Bishop, Hayley's husband, said coming up behind his wife. "I keep myself pretty fit."

She turned around and placed her hand on his arm and squeezed. "Why yes you do, and I have to admit, I like it. It doesn't seem fair; however, that I can eat whatever I want because of the baby, and you still have to watch what you eat."

"There's no way I'm going to put on sympathy weight. Do you know how hard I worked to keep my girlish figure?" he teased with a lopsided grin. Glancing over at Deanna, he asked, "You two heading out to lunch?"

"No, Deanna can't get away, so I'm going to grab take-out from Domenico's."

"Want some company? I can take a break and ride with you."

"Sure, that sounds great. It will give me a chance to go over the baby shower info with you. With Brooke and Liam's wedding coming up, I've been so busy I haven't had a chance to make sure I'm inviting everyone you want there." Hayley turned back around and waved to Deanna. "I'll be back in about an hour with lunch."

"Thanks again for picking it up for us."

"Of course; what are friends for?" Hayley said with a warm smile. "You want your usual from Domenico's?"

Deanna nodded. "Sounds great."

While there was a lull in the calls, Deanna started typing away on her keyboard. She needed to get the captain's calendar in order for the next month before the next call came in. She was only through the second week when the phone rang. She clicked the button to accept the call. "Clear Mountain Dispatch, this is Dispatcher Harper. How can I help you?"

"This is Verity over at the 9-1-1 center. We have a call for another missing hiker in your area. I'm going to forward the information. Let me know if you have any questions."

Deanna quickly checked the list of the available search and rescue officers. Aiden was already assigned to a call, but Zach and Harley, along with Ted, were available. She quickly punched Zach's number. "K-9 1, this is dispatch. We have a high priority search and rescue call for a missing hiker in the Clear Mountain area. Victim is a teenager. Mom called in worried that he was supposed to return last night, but didn't. I'm assigning you and Rescue 1 to the call."

"Copy that dispatch," Zach's voice boomed over the radio. "Show Harley and me en route. Tell Rescue 1 we'll meet him up there."

"Will do, K-9 1."

Deanna ended the call and clicked Ted's

number next. "Rescue 1, this is dispatch. You're being assigned to a new call."

Deanna went through the same information with Ted, except at the end, she added a little something extra for him. "Stay safe, Rescue 1. Don't forget we have a date tonight."

"Oh, believe me, I haven't forgotten. I can't wait. See you tonight, sweetheart."

Normally, Deanna would correct a cop if he called her that over the radio, but when Ted did it, she didn't mind. It actually made her heart flutter with affection. She wasn't sure how it happened, but she found herself smitten with Ted Hendricks.

The rest of the day passed with no further complications. Janet finally showed up right before Hayley, giving her time to spend with her friend over a late lunch. By the time she finished up, she was able to log-on and see that Zach and Ted had found the missing hiker. The young man had gotten lost and was seeking shelter in a cave.

Deanna finished up the rest of the captain's calendar before sending out a reminder email that they were having a station meeting on Wednesday. Once she was finished, she packed up her bag and got ready to leave.

Ted arrived and entered the substation from the

back. He came up and wrapped his arms around her waist as she slipped the last piece of paper into her bag. "Looking good, Dispatcher Harper."

She twisted her neck to look back at him. "You're looking pretty good yourself, Officer Hendricks."

He leaned down and placed a kiss on her lips. She let it linger there for a few moments before she reminded herself where they were and how it wouldn't be appropriate for anyone to see them like this. She pulled away, whispering, "We don't want to get caught like this. Janet could walk back in at any moment."

"I doubt it. She's in the back flirting with Tackett," he said, letting his nose nuzzle down in the crook of her neck. "We can do this for a few more moments before anyone sees us."

This time, she stepped forward and out of his reach. "Seriously, we can't do that around here."

"Why not? Everyone knows we're dating."

"Yes, but it's not professional," she corrected. "I don't want anyone we work with to think…less of us because we can't control ourselves when we're at work."

"Okay, I can't say I agree, but I respect you enough to not make you uncomfortable. I'll do my best to control myself around you…well, at least when we're at work. When we're alone and off-duty, I'm going to be all over you," he said with a wink. "Like later tonight."

"I might hold you to that, mister. For now, why don't you get out of here and get changed? I'll see you in an hour at my place when you come to pick me up."

"Yes, ma'am," he said in a mock-salute. "Anything you say, Dispatcher Harper."

He turned on his heel and playfully marched out of the room. Deanna couldn't help but watch his departing figure and think how lucky she was to be able to call him her boyfriend.

2

Clear Mountain Assembly was filled to capacity. Guests included members of the police department where Brooke worked, along with co-workers at the resort where Liam offered his sleigh rides. Many church members were also in attendance. Ted was sitting with the rest of the officers and police staff, minus the ones that were in the wedding party, which included Deanna.

She looked amazing in her royal blue bridesmaid dress. It hugged her body in all the right places. Her red curls were pinned in a fancy up-do. The outfit was completed with a sexy pair of black high heels.

"Your girl looks amazing up there," Tackett

said, leaning over and patting his friend on the back. "You're so lucky to hook up with Deanna."

"Yeah, man, don't say anything to the other guys on the team, but she's definitely the hottest one up there," Blaze added with a wink. "I bet you enjoy tapping that."

"It's not like that," Ted objected with a shake of his head. "Deanna is the real deal. She's the one."

"Does that mean you're going to propose soon then? Are you sure you want to commit, you know, with her being how she is?" Tackett asked with a raised eyebrow.

"What do you mean, 'How she is'?" Ted asked, stiffening under the obvious negative implication behind the question.

"You know, *easy*. It's how she got the job in the department, after all," Tackett explained. "I heard that she made the captain really happy to get that job."

"You should check your source. Deanna isn't like that. She's never even dated someone, let alone been with anyone from the department, until we started dating. Plus, she would never be with a married man."

"Okay," Tackett said with a shrug. "Keep telling yourself that."

Though he had heard similar rumors when he first started working at the Clear Mountain substation, it was a whole other thing to have someone whom you considered a friend repeat them to your face when you were dating the woman at the center of them. If a wedding wasn't about to start, Ted might very well have punched Tackett square in the face for the derogatory lies he was repeating about Deanna. Instead, Ted simply warned, "You should watch what you say and who you say it to, Tackett. We might have to work together, but it doesn't mean we have to be friends. If you continue to talk about my girlfriend the way you just did, I'll make sure we aren't."

"Look, Ted, I didn't mean anything by it. You just…"

The music started to play, cutting Tackett off mid-sentence. The doors opened a final time to reveal Brooke standing with the light glowing behind her. She was wearing a beautiful white satin wedding gown that cascaded down and ended just at her ankles, revealing a pair of white heels. She glided down the aisle, her white rose bouquet in her hands, until she was standing next to Liam. He reached out and took her hands in his own, his face beaming with anticipation.

Pastor Steve was standing at the front of the church and welcomed everyone. He talked about love and marriage, and how important it was to keep God as the center of it. Brooke and Liam looked happy, and Ted was glad he got to be a part of their big day by being there, especially because Brooke was an exceptional cop. On top of that, he'd gotten to know Liam over the past few months, and he was a great guy. They'd even gone horseback riding together a few times.

The ceremony sped by quickly. In short order, Brooke and Liam were married and rushing down the aisle as husband and wife. Ted watched as Deanna came by next. She lifted her hand slightly, waved towards him, and gave him an endearing smile as she passed by. He didn't care what anyone else thought. He liked Deanna and was happy to be her boyfriend. That was all that mattered.

"I'M SO HAPPY FOR YOU," Deanna gushed as she hugged her friend in the gardens of Clear Mountain Resort. "You and Liam are perfect for each other. I'm so glad I get to be a part of your special day."

"Me, too," Brooke said back, with tears in her eyes. She stepped back and looked at all of her bridesmaids. "All of you ladies have made this day so special for me. I feel so blessed to call you my friends."

"Here, let me re-apply a little powder, Brooke. You don't want to be glowing in all your photos," Erica said with a smile. "You deserve to have the best pictures ever."

The women lined back up on the side of the bride as the men filed in on the other side. The photographer started snapping pictures and telling them to change poses. As the group finished up the last of the wedding photos, all Deanna could think about was the reception and seeing Ted. As she passed by him at the wedding, she could not help but notice how handsome he looked in his navy blue suit. She had wanted to reach right out and kiss him then and there. She didn't, of course, but it had been mighty tempting. Deanna shifted back and forth on her feet, the anticipation getting worse as time went on.

"Is everything all right?" Lindsay asked, leaning forward and making sure her friend was okay. "You keep fidgeting."

Deanna could feel herself blush. She nodded

slightly, then said, "I'm fine. Just can't wait to get inside and dance."

"And see Ted," Hayley added with a smirk. "Don't forget that."

"Okay, I think we got all the photos we need out here," the wedding photographer said, glancing down at the screen of his camera. "Let me go get ready for the entrance of the bridal party before all of you come inside."

A few minutes later, the group entered the Clear Mountain Resort ballroom. There were claps and cheers as they made their way inside, but all Deanna cared about was finding Ted in the crowd. Their eyes locked, and she could tell from the smoldering look in his eyes, all he wanted to do was grab her and pull her towards him so they could kiss.

The moment was interrupted when two of the other bridesmaids grabbed Deanna by the arm and pulled her towards the head table. Spending time with Ted would just have to wait until later.

The next hour passed by with the toasts, the bouquet and garter toss, and the first dance. Afterward, the DJ invited all of the guests to join the bride and groom on the dance floor. Finally, Deanna was going to have a moment to be with Ted. He made his way around the dance floor to

Deanna's side. He reached out his hand to her. "I want nothing more than to dance with you right now."

"I want that, too," she said as she placed her hand in his and let him guide her onto the dance floor.

Deanna looked up into his brown eyes as he pulled her into his arms. They swayed to the music, enjoying the closeness the dance produced between them.

"Did I tell you how beautiful you look tonight?" Ted asked, leaning towards her, his breath tickling her ear. "I know it's bad for me to say that when we're at a wedding reception and the bride is only a few feet away. I can't help myself though; you're the most gorgeous woman in the room."

"Thank you," she said with a giggle. "You don't have to worry; your secret is safe with me. I won't tell anyone what you think."

"I don't think it; I know it. So does everyone else. The guys said the same thing earlier at the church."

The smile melted from her face as she realized the men were marginalizing her again. Ever since Deanna hit puberty and developed a curvy body, men had treated her differently. Either they tripped all over themselves when they were around her, or they thought it gave them the right to hit on her whenever and wherever they chose. Deanna hated it. She couldn't help the way she looked and wished that men saw her as more than just a woman with a large chest.

"They were commenting on how I look? Why didn't you stop them? Is it because you like them being jealous that you landed the Jessica Rabbit of the department?"

"You know about that nickname?"

She nodded, her eyes narrowing in anger. "Of course I do. I'm not stupid. I've heard the guys talk. I wish they didn't refer to me like that, but I don't see it changing any time soon."

"For the record, whenever they've said something like that in front of me, I've always stopped them, even before you were my girlfriend. I don't like it when guys treat women like that, especially when they aren't there to defend themselves."

"I appreciate that," Deanna said, relaxing in his arms again. "I know I shouldn't punish you because of what they say. It's not your fault. It's just a sore subject for me. I've had to deal with it ever since I entered junior high school."

"That's not fair. I'm sorry you've had that happen to you. You deserve better than that."

"You two need to stop looking so serious," Liam said, leaning over from his spot on the dance floor with his new wife. "This is a party after all, and you need to be having fun."

"Agreed," Brooke said. "Whatever you two are discussing, I demand you stop at once and focus on the Electric Slide, which is going to start…right about…now," she said with a laugh, just as the familiar music started to play.

Everyone formed rows on the dance floor, following the instructions of the dance. All the dancers took four steps to their right, then four side steps to the left. Next, they took two steps to the back, then a step-touch where they stepped back on one foot and tapped their other foot in place. The final step was the pivot and brush where the whole group moved ninety degrees to the left and started the whole process over again.

After about ten rounds, Deanna was out of breath and giddy from all the excitement. She glanced over at Ted, who had also gotten into the dance. He had a giant grin on his face as he grabbed her hand and pulled her off the dance floor. "I think I need a drink after that. Care to join me?"

She nodded, letting him continue to guide her over to the nearby bar. He ordered them both a drink, then handed one of the glasses to her.

"I can't believe how much fun that was," Ted admitted as he took a sip of his drink. "I've never done that before."

"Are you serious? What about at other weddings?"

He shook his head.

"What about at bars? Cruises? Proms?"

He shook his head for each one, causing Deanna to be more and more perplexed with each shake. "Why not?"

"I haven't done any of those. Well, I mean, I've been a guest at a couple of other weddings, but I managed to stay off the dance floor."

"What about the other places I mentioned?" she asked, taking a sip of her drink.

"I'm not a big bar guy, I've never been on a cruise, and I didn't go to my prom."

"You didn't go to prom?" Deanna asked in incredulousness, nearly spitting her soda out of her mouth. She knew her reaction was over the top, but she couldn't help herself. "Prom is a rite of passage. How could you not go?"

"Well, my girlfriend of three years had just broken up with me, and I didn't feel like taking some random girl with me. Besides, we'd bought our tickets together. It didn't seem right to go when we weren't together anymore. I gave my ticket to one of her friends, instead."

"That was really nice of you, Ted."

"The kicker though, was she ended up using my ticket to take the guy she dumped me for. I didn't even find out until after prom night was over when one of my friends told me."

"Oh no, Ted, that must have really stung."

"It definitely added salt to the wound, that's for sure. Maybe that's why I haven't danced since that night. Never wanted to until now…with you."

Deanna was touched by the kind admission. She knew Ted cared about her, but when he said things like that, it really reinforced it. "Well, I'm glad you did. As a matter of fact, why don't we go out and do it some more? Consider tonight your official do-over prom." Deanna reached out and grabbed his hand, ready to spend the night making this the best night of Ted's life.

3

Today was the day. They were ready. Ted decided he couldn't put it off any longer. He was going to ask the captain about letting him work with Titan on the rescue team starting this week.

Ted marched inside the substation with Titan by his side. His co-workers were surprised to see him there on his day off—especially with his dog by his side—but Ted figured this was the best way to plead his case.

Deanna wasn't at her desk. He planned it that way since he didn't want to get her in trouble if this didn't go his way. He figured it gave her plausible deniability if she was at her dentist appointment.

He knocked on the captain's door. A couple of moments later, he heard him bark out, "Come in."

Ted entered the office to find Captain McGregor behind his oak desk. He glanced up and asked, "What are you doing here today, Ted? It's your day off." He glanced at Titan with a puzzled look on his face. "Why did you bring your pet?"

"He's not my pet," Ted clarified. "I'm hoping you'll let him be my new partner."

Captain McGregor stood up from his chair and came around to stand in front of them. "What's this all about?"

"This is Titan. He worked search and rescue in Boulder before his partner died in a car accident. No one wanted to partner with Titan after his death and the officer had no family to take him. They put out an offer for someone in the department to adopt him."

"I still don't see what that has to do with you and our substation," Captain McGregor stated, glancing down at the German shepherd.

"I know Titan still has a lot of good years of police work left in him. I adopted him and have spent my off-time training with him. He's good, Captain; I mean really good, and we work well together. I even took him to several K9 trials around the country, and we've won every competition we've been in." Ted released Titan from his leash, and gave him several commands to show he knew all of their departmental procedures. "I even adapted him to snow and ice terrain this past winter."

"I can see you put a lot of time and effort into this, and that he's a good police dog. We aren't looking, however, to hire a third K9 team."

"I know that, Captain, but we could be a real asset to the search and rescue division."

"I'm not arguing that, Ted, but we can't afford another K9 handler and the upkeep of another dog."

"I can keep my same title and pay, and I'll cover all the costs of Titan's upkeep. I just want to be able to use him on the job," Ted pleaded, hoping that the offer would make the difference.

"I really wish I could say yes, Ted. I know how much you want to be a K9 handler, but I just can't do it. We can't afford the liability of another dog. If he bites someone, the department will be liable for it. There's no way around it. I'm sorry, but it just can't happen."

Ted wanted to argue, but he could see from his captain's resolute expression, it wouldn't do any good. His superior's mind was made up on the matter.

Ted nodded, then bent down, re-attaching the

leash to Titan's collar. "Thanks for hearing me out, Captain."

"Maybe in a couple of years as the town grows, things will be different," his captain explained, "and you will be at the top of the list for the next K9 position."

As Ted and Titan exited the office, deep disappointment settled into Ted's heart. He didn't have a couple of years to wait around to possibly get a K9 slot. He wasn't getting any younger, and the job was extremely demanding. He only had a few years left before he needed to move behind a desk. If he wanted to be a K9 handler before he retired, he was going to have to move on to plan B.

"What are you doing here? Did you come to surprise me? I thought we weren't getting together until tonight," Deanna said as she got out of her car in the substation parking lot. She came over to Ted's car where he was loading up Titan into his kennel. "What's Titan doing here with you?" She reached out and rubbed Titan between his ears.

"We came to talk to the captain." Ted didn't elaborate on what that meant, but he could tell from Deanna's face she already knew.

Despite that, she asked, "How did it go? What did he say?"

"Not great. Looks like Titan's going to stay my 'pet' as the captain put it."

"I'm so sorry, Ted. I know how bad you wanted this."

"I just don't get it. I feel like this was what I was called to do. I thought it was a sign when Titan became available for adoption. We clicked so well; right from the beginning. I thought the captain would see that and realize it was worth the extra effort."

"You have to remember; he has a boss to report to like the rest of us. He has to make the numbers work."

"I know, I just thought we could figure out a way. I guess I was wrong." He gestured to Titan, latching the kennel. "Let me get him home and change. I'll pick you up at six at your place."

She nodded. "See you then."

He leaned over and gave her a quick kiss on the lips before climbing into his truck. He headed home where he decided to start on plan B right away. He pulled out his laptop and started a search for open K9 positions in the US. He didn't want to move away from his friends and family, and especially Deanna, but if he ever wanted to be a K9 handler, it might be the only way. There were a couple of open spots back East as well as one in Iowa. He bookmarked all of them, debating about if he wanted to live in places like that. He was about to turn off his computer when at the bottom of the list, he saw an opening for his dream job. He almost couldn't believe his eyes. Was it possible?

K9 SEARCH AND RESCUE HANDLER FOR POSITION AT PRESTIGIOUS TRAINING ACADEMY

Disaster City Search and Rescue Academy is currently seeking a K9 Handler to be trained and hired to work at our academy in the specialized terrain division. Qualified handler will possess characteristics and traits, such as patience, self-discipline, and attention to detail. The handler must be of unquestionable integrity and exercise good judgment. The handler must be willing and able to teach incoming students via the academy's techniques and procedures once learned through our academy.

Required Schedule: Minimum 40 Hours Per week; may be required to work additional hours as needed.

Handler and K9 will live and work at the academy in Texas. All care and maintenance for handler and K9 will be maintained at the facility.

Personnel must have a minimum of four years of documented successful experience in law enforcement or military service. Additionally, applicant must be a certified Search and Rescue handler.

Applicant must undergo all screenings to successfully pass government background checks in order to work certain areas during national calls. Must pass all physical requirements for the position.

Scope of Work:

- *EMPLOYEE shall complete the tasks, obligations, and responsibilities as a K9 instructor for the academy once trained. K9 Handlers are to work as part of an instruction team once graduated. The K9 Handler performs his or her duties while commanding a trained working dog that has met certification standards.*

General Duties and Responsibilities:

- *EMPLOYEE will be fluid and flexible in adapting to rapidly changing situations.*
- *EMPLOYEE may be required to assist in operational tasks such as supervision, logistics, administration and training, if and when, requested by his or her chain-of-command.*
- *EMPLOYEE must, at all times, follow the rules and guidelines of the academy.*

Ted was glad that before he did his K9 trials, he applied and received his certification as a handler. Titan's certification hadn't expired when Ted adopted him, and was still active. Even though they hadn't officially served on a department together, they were both qualified individually. He hoped the awards they won during the half dozen K9 trials would prove they were the perfect search and rescue team. He figured it was worth filling out the application for his dream job. He probably wouldn't get the job, but he would always wonder if he didn't at least try for it.

An hour later, he clicked the send button. His resume and application were being delivered via email. He wasn't sure if they would even take him seriously, but his Army friend Adam Reynolds had gone there for training and got a job, so he figured anything was possible.

Having a sense of accomplishment after working towards his career goal, Ted spent the rest of his time getting ready for his date with Deanna. He quickly showered and slipped on a pair of jeans and a button-up, ready to have a good time with his girlfriend now that he had a plan.

Two weeks later.

DEANNA WAS EXCITED to go out with Ted tonight. He told her via text he had big news. She hoped that it meant a proposal was forthcoming. Considering they had been dating exclusively for over a year now, she was ready to settle down and start a family with him.

She took a final look in the mirror to make sure her knee-length, form-fitting little black dress was wrinkle-free and laying just right along her curves. She fluffed her curls and touched up her mauve lipstick before leaving her bedroom.

Just as she arrived in her living room, she heard a knock at the door. She rushed over and opened it. "Hold on just a second while I grab my coat and purse."

Ted let out a chuckle. "Guess I should be used to this."

"What can I say, I'm always running behind."

He helped her into her cream coat, then she closed and locked her door. "Where are we going?"

"I have reservations for us at Sushi Mon over at the Riverwalk," Ted said as he opened his truck door for her. He helped her inside as he added, "I know it's your favorite."

"I love how fancy all the different rolls look, especially the ones that come out on fire."

"Do you remember the first time you tried to blow one out and they explained you had to let the fire die out so it would cook the roll?"

She let out a laugh. "Yes, I nearly burnt the restaurant down by doing it. I thought for sure they would never let me come back."

Ted climbed into the truck beside Deanna, then turned the key in the ignition. "No; my sincere apology, not to mention a hefty tip, smoothed things over with the owner. Now they love us."

"Thank goodness, because they really do have the best sushi in town."

"Well, it's not like there's a lot of competition. There really is only one other sushi place in Clear Mountain."

After a short ten-minute ride over, they arrived at the Riverwalk, which was bustling with tons of locals as well as tourists who frequented the place. It was a favorite hangout spot in the town for both couples and families alike, who spent their time shopping, dining, and walking along the concrete boardwalk.

The hostess guided them to their usual table by the window. Deanna enjoyed watching the people walk by on the boardwalk, and it pleased her to know Ted remembered.

"Welcome to Sushi Mon. Your server will be right with you," the pretty brunette said as she handed them both a menu. A moment later, she turned around and headed back to the front of the restaurant.

"Are we going to get our usual?" Deanna asked, glancing through the menu out of curiosity to see if they'd added anything new.

"We can do that, but first, I need to talk with you about something."

Deanna's mouth suddenly went dry. She set down her menu, then placed her hands in her lap. She discreetly rubbed her palms on the edge of her dress to keep them from sweating, wanting them to be perfect for when he took her hand and popped the question.

"You know how I've talked about the Disaster City Search and Rescue Academy, right?"

She nodded. "Only about a million times." She wanted to question what that had to do with him proposing, but she figured he would get to the point in a minute.

"Well, they were hiring a new search and rescue K9 handler to train and be given a position as an instructor at the academy. I mean, it's everything I have ever dreamed of. Beyond instruction, they also handle calls for service near the academy, send teams to national disasters, and work with relief efforts across the globe. When I saw the position was open, I decided I had to apply. I honestly didn't think I had a real shot, but I figured it couldn't hurt to try for it. Adam Reynolds, my friend from the Army base, texted me and told me he put in a good word for me. I guess between his recommendation and the awards I've won on the job here in Clear Mountain, plus at the various K9 trials, prompted them to offer me the position."

Deanna's eyes grew wide with astonishment. Did she just hear him right? Was he telling her that he was considering taking a job several states away? What did that mean for them? Did he bring her here to break up with her? She pressed her lips together, contemplating how to make sense of all of this.

"I know this must come as a shock, and I would have told you sooner if I actually thought there was a chance I would get the job. I half did it out of spite because of what the captain told me."

Deanna let out a heavy sigh, then shook her head. "I don't know what to say, Ted."

"Tell me you understand why I did it."

"I can't honestly say that. I thought you were happy here. Your family is here, your job is here, your friends are here, I'm here."

"I am happy here, minus the job. I want to be a K9 handler. It's all I've ever wanted to be, but if I wait for a spot to possibly become available here, I might lose the chance altogether. The academy is my dream job. I would be a fool to pass it up."

"It sounds like you've already made up your mind then. I guess if we're not enough, then you have to go after what makes you happy," Deanna said, trying to sound supportive, but knowing she sounded bitter despite her best efforts. "No matter what it costs you in the process."

"I'm hoping it won't cost me anything. I care about you, Deanna, and I'm hoping you'd be willing to try a long-distance relationship with me."

She glanced down at her hands, wishing she hadn't spent the money on the manicure. She'd thought Ted would be slipping a ring on her finger tonight, not telling her he was moving away for a job she didn't even know existed. She had wanted her hand to look perfect for the pictures she planned to post on social media afterward. Now, it seemed so silly. None of that was going to happen.

Instead, she had to wrap her head around the idea of dealing with a long-distance relationship. They never seemed to last, but she cared about Ted and didn't want to give up on what they had together. Plus, she'd already invested a year into the relationship. Was she willing to walk away from that, from him?

Deanna shook her head and tried to push back the tears that were threatening to fall. How did this happen? Why hadn't she seen it coming when the captain refused to make Ted a K9 handler? She should have known he would go looking for a job elsewhere, since it was all he'd ever wanted to do.

"What's wrong? You look upset."

"I'm just worried, Ted. This is a lot of pressure to put on our relationship. You're going to be moving and starting a new job. Working with new people in a new environment. Can you handle all of that and still have time for me, for us? I don't want to be an added burden for you."

"You'd never be a burden for me, Deanna. I mean it, I want us to make this work. Tell me you do, too."

Deanna pushed away her concerns and plastered on her most charming smile. "Of course, I do, Ted. You know me, I can do anything if I set my mind to it. Why should this be any different? I'll find a way to make it work like I always do."

Even as she said the words, she wondered if she believed them. Ted might very well be the love of her life, but she wasn't sure if that was enough to withstand what the future held for them.

4

Ted couldn't believe his eyes as he drove through the gates of the Disaster City Search and Rescue grounds. The facility was massive, with multiple huge buildings set on a vast amount of land. He wasn't sure how much, but he would guess at least twenty acres based off his family's ranch.

He pulled his truck up and climbed out. He came around to the back and helped Titan out of his kennel. It had been a long drive down from Colorado, but it was easier than flying.

"I'm guessing you must be Ted Hendricks," a deep Southern accent with a long drawl said from behind him.

Ted spun around to find a tall, lanky man with brown hair and steely blue eyes staring at him. He was leaning against a light pole in a casual way, but Ted got the distinct feeling, despite the accent and demeanor, the man was anything but relaxed.

"I'm Officer Jesse Dixon, one of the specialized terrain instructors for urban and natural disasters. You're one of my new recruits. Why don't you follow me?"

Ted didn't need to be asked twice. He quickly followed behind the other man, who kept a fast and steady pace as they walked across the parking lot into the administration building.

"We had you arrive here early so that we could get you orientated before the rest of your class shows up. They are going through the academy as standard trainees, but you are here to train with the specific goal of becoming one of our instructors. That means we will be paying special attention to you and expecting more out of you. If you don't measure up, not only will you fail to graduate, but you won't be offered the position of instructor and team member. I hope you thrive in high-stress situations, because this will be the most difficult month of your life."

Ted followed Officer Dixon through a maze of halls until they reached an office that was filled with two other men. They were standing in a row in their blue cargo Disaster City Search and Rescue uniforms.

"This is Officer Terrance Bilmont," he gestured to the taller of the two men, "and Joe Griffin. When and if you graduate, you will be working with the three of us directly. In the meantime, we will be overseeing your training."

Terrance Bilmont was a big man with dark features. He towered over Ted, even with his six-foot frame. The other man moved towards Ted, narrowing his brown eyes into slits. "Are you ready for this, Trainee?"

Ted nodded. "Yes, Sir."

"We don't use *sir* around here. It's Instructor Bilmont, Trainee."

"You have some mighty big shoes to fill, Trainee," said the shorter black-haired man with gray eyes and a thick New York accent. "Rick Buckworth was a legend among K9 handlers, and he will be missed. If you want to end up being half the handler and a quarter of the instructor he was, you will pay close attention to everything we say."

Ted was aware they were trying to use the standard tactic of fear to see if they could shake him. What they didn't know was that Ted was unshakeable. He was known around the Clear Mountain Search and Rescue team as having nerves of steel. Nothing phased him.

"Understood," Ted said with resolve. "I will prove it wasn't a mistake to hire me."

"You mean to take a chance on you?" Instructor Dixon questioned. "Because that's what we're doing. You're lucky you have friends on the staff here, Trainee. Otherwise, we would have probably passed right over your application."

Ted wasn't sure what to think about that information. He was grateful Adam put in a good word for him, but he had hoped his resume also made a good impression. Had that not been the case? Was he only here because of his friend?

Determined not to let them see Dixon's words affected him, Ted continued to keep his reaction from showing. He had half-hoped his friend would have been there to greet him, but considering how they were already acting like he was only there because of his friend, he was glad that hadn't happened. He wanted to prove that he and Titan deserved this position.

"I'm going to finish showing you the rest of the

facility, and then I suggest you get some rest. Tomorrow the rest of the recruits will be arriving, and you will see why this place trains the best of the best as they reveal their pedigrees. Any one of them might make a better impression on us. We could change our minds and offer them your job. Just remember that, Trainee," Dixon said, as he gestured for Ted to follow after him.

An hour later, Ted had visited the whole place, which in all reality was an all-inclusive mini-city. From the kennels to the veterinarian hospital, from the medical clinic to the state-of-the-art gym and pool, the place had everything. They toured the cafeteria, the auditorium, and the training center with classrooms and staff offices. The only places they didn't make it to were the various training grounds spread across the outskirts of the campus. He would get to see those with the other trainees once the academy started.

"We also have male and female dormitories for trainees, which is where you will be staying for the duration of your time in the academy. You can either keep your K9 partner with you, or house him at the kennel. We leave that up to each trainee. *If* you graduate and get offered the instructor position, you will be given an apartment in the staff villa," Dixon explained. They stopped in front of the male dormitory. "You'll see your name on your room door. Inside, you will find your uniforms, schedule, and curriculum. I suggest you prepare yourself for the start of the academy on Monday. It promises to be a long day."

Ted entered his room, which was really more of a tiny apartment with a small living area, bedroom, and bathroom. Titan seemed right at home, finding a spot near the edge of the couch and plopping down. Ted wanted nothing more than to do the same on the couch, but he knew he had way too much to do if he wanted to make a good impression. He walked over to the small desk in the corner of the room. All of the information Dixon mentioned was there. He flipped through it, trying to figure out where he was going to start. School had never been his strong suit.

He felt a buzzing in his jeans' pocket. He reached in and pulled out his phone. It was a text from Deanna.

Did you arrive safely? How is it going? Do you like the other guys there?

Ted thought about his answer for several

seconds. How was it going? What did he think of the instructors? If he was honest, he felt overwhelmed, but he wasn't sure he wanted to admit that to Deanna. That would just make her think she was right about him coming here. Instead, he texted back what he thought he should say.

Arrived safe. Everything is fine. Have a lot to do before tomorrow.

She texted back immediately:

You have time for a video chat?

He responded:

Can I have a rain check for tomorrow? Exhausted from the drive. Want to go over the info and then take a hot shower before bed.

There was a bit of a longer pause this time. Then she finally texted back:

Okay. Have a good night. Praying for you.

Immediately, Ted felt bad for not accepting her offer to chat. Before he could change his mind though, there was a knock at the door. He went over and opened it up to find Adam on the other side.

"Man, am I glad to see you," Ted said with relief. "It's good to see a friendly smile."

"That bad, huh?" Adam said with a shake of his head. "Don't worry. They're always tough on new recruits like that, particularly ones that stand to be instructors at the end."

"I know; I get it. Doesn't make it easier, though. You want to come in?"

Adam shrugged, then entered the room. "Sure; I mean I don't want to keep you from doing what you need to do. I just wanted to stop by and let you know I'm here for you. I mean, I can't really hang out much because they frown on trainee/instructor fraternizing, but I think since your class hasn't even started yet, this doesn't count."

"Plus, you're used to breaking that rule, right, Adam? Isn't that how you ended up dating your current girlfriend who happens to be an instructor here at the academy?"

"Hey now, no need to call me out like that, but yes, I ended up with Clara by breaking the fraternizing rule. Best decision of my life, by the way. I ended up with the best girl and the best job in the world."

"I don't know. My girl, Deanna, is pretty amazing. She let me come here, after all."

"That is a tall order. You're lucky she's so supportive. Make sure to hang on to her."

Ted nodded "I plan to."

"What do you have left to do tonight?" Adam asked, looking around the room.

"I have to go over the information on the desk. They made it sound like a suggestion, but I've been through enough academies to know that suggestions are never really just that."

"You're right on that. Take whatever you've been through in a normal academy, and magnify it by ten, and you'll be close to what Disaster City demands of you." Adam moved over to the desk and glanced down at the books. "I can help you with this, if you like. Sometimes it helps to have someone go over it with you."

"You'd do that?"

"Like I said, your class hasn't officially started yet, so I don't see how this would be breaking the rules." Adam picked up one of the books and headed over to the couch. "Let's start with this one. You just need to familiarize yourself with the sections. They won't expect you to know more than that at the beginning."

Ted took a spot next to Adam on the couch, grateful that his friend was there to help him. He knew he couldn't depend on Adam all the time, but even for this brief window of opportunity, Ted was glad he wasn't alone.

THE BACK ROOM of Domenico's was filled with twenty of Hayley Hall Bishop's closest friends, female co-workers, and church members as well as her mother. Deanna had made sure to send a personal invitation to each of them, wanting her best friend's baby shower to be perfect.

As each guest entered the room, Deanna handed them a paper cup filled with a baby in ice. She explained that it was for the game, "Ice, Ice, Baby," where each guest would hold onto their plastic mini-baby that was frozen in a paper cup. When one of the guests warmed their baby enough to break free from the ice, they would win.

Daphne, the pastor's wife, entered the room next. Deanna handed her one of the ice cups and explained the rules of the game.

"You did a wonderful job planning this, Deanna. Hayley is lucky to have a good friend like you."

"Thank you, Daphne. That means a lot coming from you."

"I absolutely love all the decorations."

Pink was everywhere, from the tablecloths, to the balloons spread around the room, to the banner that read, *Welcome Baby Addie.* Deanna also had a clothesline of pink baby items on one wall and a diaper cake in the center of the gift table, which was filling up with stacks of pink and purple presents covered in teddy bears, ballerinas, and baby animals.

The baby shower had been a welcome distraction from lingering on what was going on with Ted. She'd been so busy planning the shower, she hadn't had time to dwell on his departure, or how lonely she felt now that he was gone. He'd only been away a few days, but it felt like an eternity. What worried her most though, was what happened if he made it through the academy and they offered him the job? It would mean he would be staying in Texas permanently, and she couldn't see how they would make that work.

Hayley came over and wrapped her arms around Deanna, bringing her back to the present. She pulled her into a hug as best she could with her nearly nine-month pregnant belly sticking out between them. "Thank you for doing all of this, Deanna. I feel so special."

"Good, that was the whole idea," Deanna said with a smile. "This is all about you and that beautiful baby girl I can't wait to meet in just a few more weeks."

"I can't believe you had the time to do all of this," she said, looking around the room in awe. "You put so much detail into everything. I love the pink and white candy bar."

Deanna glanced over at the area she was talking about to make sure none of the candy in the dozen glass jars of various designs and sizes were running low. Relief flooded her when she realized that though the women were eating the candy, it seemed she had picked the right ones for each. Plenty were left in them.

"I saw it on a Pinterest board and knew how much you love candy. I thought it would be perfect."

"I love it especially right now. It seems all she wants is sweets."

"So, the cliché is true?" Erica asked, coming up to them. "Little girls want sweets because they are made of sugar and spice, and everything nice?"

Hayley let out a chuckle and shook her head. "I'm not sure about that. This little one sure likes to throw a little naughty in there by kicking the crud out of my rib cage in the middle of the night, not to mention the indigestion she causes on a regular basis."

"Wow! That makes a girl want to stay clear of having a baby. I might have to tell Zach babies are off the table," Erica said with her eyes rounding with aversion.

"It's not all bad though," Lindsay said, coming up to the group. "You also melt the moment you hear the baby's heartbeat over the speakers at the doctor's office, or when you see their face on the ultrasound. Plus, you can't beat the pure joy you feel when they move inside you for the first time."

"She's right," Hayley agreed. "Despite all the little annoyances, this has been the best experience of my life. I wouldn't trade it for anything."

Deanna glanced around the room, counting the guests. Once she confirmed everyone was present, she moved towards the front of the room. "Welcome, everyone, to Hayley's baby shower. I'm glad all of you could come today and be a part of this special day for Hayley. I figured we could play a few games to start off our time. Feel free to help yourself to the buffet and the candy bar while we play."

They started out with a game of Blind Blocking. She had two guests at a time sit down at an empty table. They were blindfolded and asked to stack blocks as best they could. Whoever stacked them all, or the most, in the one-minute time frame, won that round. Then the winner of each round would go against each other until there was a champion. It turned out, Stacy Wingate, from church, was really good at stacking blocks, which was surprising considering she was one of the oldest guests at the party. For her prize, Deanna gave her a gift card to the Riverwalk to use at any of the stores.

The next game was "Sugar Baby." Gummy letters that spelled out the word B-A-B-Y were hidden in two bowls of sugar and the guests had to use a plastic spoon in their mouths to fish them out of the bowl. Apparently, Lindsay was really good at doing it, because she beat all the competitors, winning round after round. At the end, she was declared the winner and Deanna gave her a wrapped coffee mug as a prize.

The final game was more relaxed. Deanna carried out a tray filled with baby items and had the guests look at them quickly, trying to memorize as many items as they could. She removed the tray from the room, and the participants had to write down as many as they could remember. Once they were done, she brought the tray back into the room and Hayley held up each item, which she got to keep, and named them. Brooke won this one. Apparently, her time as a detective really paid off, because she was the only one to memorize all twenty items on the tray.

Just as Deanna was handing Brooke her prize, a gift card to Superior Coffee, there was a squeal of surprise from across the room. "Oh, I broke my water," Erica shouted, jumping up from her chair. Everyone turned to look at her with shocked faces. Quickly, they all realized she was talking about the baby in the ice game. "Does this mean I won?"

Everyone started to laugh at her funny reaction. Deanna went over and handed Brooke a wrapped candle as her prize for winning, patting her on the back. "Good job."

After the games were finished, it was time for Hayley to open her presents. As she pulled out each of the baby gifts, the guests cooed over how adorable the clothes were, and how there were so many new things to help with raising babies.

They finished off the afternoon with some cake and chit-chat. The guests slowly said their good-byes, leaving Deanna and her closest friends behind.

"Can we help you clean up?" Lindsay offered, pulling her blonde hair up into a ponytail.

"You don't have to," Deanna rebuffed.

"We want to," Erica added, putting her own black hair up in a bun. "You shouldn't have to take care of all of this by yourself."

"Thanks," she said with a smile. "I'd like the company."

The women began the process of cleaning up. As they did, they talked about their jobs and relationships. It only took a few minutes before the conversation turned towards Deanna.

"How's it going with Ted being in Texas?" Erica asked with concern. "Have you gotten a chance to talk with him much since he arrived at the academy?"

Deanna shook her head. "He's been settling in and really busy."

"Oh well, I'm sure it will get easier," Erica said with a sympathetic smile.

"Yes, I remember when I was transferring from Boulder over to Clear Mountain for my detective position. It was really hard for me to find the time for Liam like I had before," Brooke explained as she packed away the candy bar. "It got better though."

"Yes, and while you're figuring everything out, you have us," Lindsay added, reaching out and squeezing her friend's hand. "We're here for you, no matter what."

"I'm sure you're all right. Things will settle down once he gets into a routine at the academy," Deanna said, pretending it didn't bother her having him so far away and not knowing what was going on with her boyfriend. She missed him so much and wondered if he was feeling the same way. Did absence make the heart grow fonder, or was Ted so busy she didn't even cross his mind?

The women finished up getting everything packed back into the boxes, then helped Hayley carry her gifts to her Honda Accord. Once the items were safely stowed in the trunk and back seat, the other women said their goodbyes, leaving Hayley and Deanna alone.

"I didn't want to say anything around everyone else, but since Ted's focusing on his career right now, maybe it's time you finally start looking at your own. You've put your dreams of being a cop on the back burner for long enough. I think you should apply to police academies."

"It's been too long, Hayley. What's the point? I'm good at my job and content."

Hayley shook her head. "You just don't want to disappoint anyone, but you have every right to pursue your own dreams. It's never too late for that. Just promise me you'll think about it."

Deanna didn't want to argue with her friend. Instead, she simply nodded before giving her a hug goodbye. Deanna wasn't sure what the future held for her, but Hayley was right about one thing, she needed to consider what a life without Ted might look like.

5

The anticipation of the first day of training was causing Ted to overthink everything. He checked and re-checked his uniform, making sure it was pressed perfectly and his boots were polished so bright he could see his face in them. He also checked Titan to make sure he was ready for his first day, giving him extra water, filling his pocket with treats, and making sure his collar and vest were on properly.

Even though Ted had impeccable training at Clear Mountain Search and Rescue, and Titan had been expertly trained in Boulder, they were both here to learn from the best of the best in the search and rescue world.

Ted glanced down at his watch, making sure he

had plenty of time to get over to the auditorium for the first day orientation. If he left now, he would be there a few minutes early, just the way he liked it. He arrived with a group of other trainees. They all made their way inside and took seats in the large room.

Once the room was full, Ted did a head count and realized there were 60 total trainees, fifty-four men and six women. On the stage, there were twenty instructors—all men including Adam with the exception of one woman, Adam's girlfriend, Clara—standing in two rows. Two other men, their insignias on their uniforms making it clear they were in charge, stood to the side of them.

Ted wasn't surprised by the lack of women in the room. There were significantly fewer female officers in law enforcement, and it was even more rare to see one as a K9 handler.

A middle-aged man with salt-and-peppered brown hair came forward. "Welcome, trainees, to the elite Disaster City Search and Rescue Academy, better known as DCSRA. I'm Master Sergeant Trevor Young, commander of this esteemed institution."

The commander went over the layout of the

facility, the rules and guidelines, and the expectations while the trainees were there.

"Because we offer all these conveniences, you need to understand it means you have no excuse to underperform. Each of you should meet our high standards to graduate from our academy. A select few may even exceed our expectations, but I promise you, it will be hard to do that. This class may only be a month long, but it'll be the most intense time of your life. It will test your limits, challenge what you think you know about search and rescue, and put you in situations you've never considered. Next, you will be hearing from Officer Ben Miller, second-in-command here at DCSRA. He will be directly in charge of your training and will introduce the rest of the staff here at the academy."

A thickly built man with black hair and dark eyes came to the front of the auditorium. He looked to be a little bit older than Ted, but it was clear he took his job seriously from the stern look on his face. "As the sergeant explained, as the deputy commander, I will be in charge of making sure each of you master the top techniques and skills taught by our highly-qualified instructors. By the time you finish your time at DCSRA, you'll be the best search and rescue officers and soldiers in the world." He gestured to the rows of men and one woman behind him. "We have six sections of S & R with two instructors per division, plus an additional eight instructors assigned to specialized areas. You may think the low instructor to trainee ratio will work to your benefit, that you'll receive tons of hands-on guidance by the most elite teacher in your field, which is true. What you also need to realize is that it also means all eyes will be on you. If you mess up, we'll see it. If you slack off, we'll see it. If you break our rules, we'll see it.

"Officer Reggie Collins and Staff Sergeant Alex Murray provide training for missing persons, Sergeant Major Juan Perez and Officer Paul Smithen run cadaver training, Officer John Lee and Gunnery Sergeant Justin Ford handle tracking and scouting, Officer Clara Burnette and Staff Sergeant Adam Reynolds oversee bomb detection, Officers Sean West and Dylan Burke handle patrol and sentry training, and Officers Matthew Knight and Ray Carlson are in charge of narcotics training. The seven instructors oversee specialized terrain training; Mason Fredericks and Tom Powell train at the lake for water rescue while Officer Ross Canter and Master Sergeant James Franklin train in the nearby mountains for avalanche and snow conditions. Finally, Officers Jesse Dixon, Joe Griffin, and Terrance Bilmont oversee urban disasters such as terrorist attacks, as well as natural disasters which include mudslides, wildfires, and earthquakes."

The deputy commander spent the remaining time going over the other staff members at the facility and the schedule for the rest of the day. Once they were finished, they were dismissed for lunch before they started their initial training in the afternoon.

Inside the cafeteria, you could have heard a pin drop from how quiet everyone was. Though the trainees were sitting with each other, they weren't talking. A few minutes later, the staff came in and made their way to a few of the empty back tables. They didn't seem to have any reservation about talking and laughing amongst themselves. Ted noticed that several of the other trainees looked over, as if debating whether it meant they could talk. After several minutes, they slowly started doing so. Soon a soft hum of chattering could be heard in the room.

"Let me be the first to introduce myself. I'm Kenneth Daniels. I'm an officer with Boston PD and here for narcotics training," the young blond man with a friendly smile said.

"Nice to meet you, Kenneth," Ted said with a nod of his head. "I'm Officer Ted Hendricks. I was with Clear Mountain Search and Rescue out of Colorado before coming here to train for the specialized terrain division, specifically natural disasters."

"I'm going to be in specialized terrain, too. I'm Special Agent Mark Turano. The FBI sent me here for terrorist disaster training," said the burly, middle-aged, auburn-haired man with a beard sitting across from them.

The final brown-haired man at the table took a little longer to introduce himself. He spoke with a Southern drawl and a small stutter. "I'm Will B-Burdue, from the New Orleans Police Department. I was s-sent here to train for bomb detection."

"My friend, Adam Reynolds, heads up bomb detection. He's a good guy," Ted said with a grin. "You couldn't have a better instructor."

"Glad to h-hear that," Will said with relief in his brown eyes.

The handlers spent the rest of the time talking about their most memorable assignments in search and rescue, and before they knew it, lunch time was over. Mark and Ted decided they would walk together with their K9 partners over to the classrooms since they were in the same division. They entered the room marked disasters to find Officers Joe Griffin, Terrance Bilmont and Jesse Dixon standing at the front of the room. As the trainees entered the room, they gestured for them to take seats.

Once the clock struck one, Instructor Bilmont went to the back and shut the door while Instructor Griffin spoke to the group. "Good afternoon, trainees, welcome to your first day at the most prestigious and elite urban and natural disaster search and rescue school in the world. All of you have been hand-selected to train here because you are the best in your departments, but what you need to know is that means nothing here. Here, you are starting out from scratch. You will do things our way—which is the best and only way. No matter how good you think you are at search and rescue, no matter how many rewards you've won or lives you've saved," he looked directly at Ted and paused for a moment, "none of that means anything here. Here, there is only one thing that matters. Our house, our rules. What that means is everything you think you know, what you've learned and used as a handler, doesn't matter here. DCSRA is the best of the best, which means we don't want to hear anything you have to say. We don't need to hear about your expertise or techniques, because none of what you know is near good enough to surpass what the three of us know about disaster training."

Their instructors didn't miss a beat. They started right in on going over their expectations and requirements. Ted pulled out his notepad and pen, taking down notes so he wouldn't forget anything. By the end of the first day, he was exhausted. As he made his way back to his dorm to get ready for dinner, he got a text from Deanna.

How did your first day go?

He thought about his answer. School had never been easy for him, and with the amount of book-work required, he wondered if he would be able to cut it. He knew, however, he had nowhere else to go if this didn't work out. He had given his notice to his Clear Mountain captain, certain that his future was at DCSRA.

Harder than I thought, but I'm making it work.

She texted back:

You want to talk about it?

Though part of him wanted to accept the offer, he was so tired all he wanted to do was grab some dinner, finish the written assignment, and go to sleep.

Rain check. Give me a couple of days to get used to my routine and we can do a video date.

There was a long pause before she texted back a final time.

Okay. Just know I'm praying for you. TTYS

Ted felt bad about his response to Deanna. He could tell she wasn't happy about it. He had to remind himself that as hard as it was for him to be here, it was equally hard for her to be left back there without him. Silently, he sent up a prayer asking God to help him succeed both at the academy and as a boyfriend. He didn't want to fail at either job.

TWO DAYS HAD PASSED since Ted started the academy. Deanna had given Ted the space he needed to get used to being there. She was excited when he texted her and said he had some free time Wednesday evening and wanted to claim that video date with her.

Deanna had picked out the perfect outfit—a pair of skinny jeans and a cream sweater. The outfit looked casual at first glance but also enhanced her features enough that she hoped Ted would notice.

Her laptop buzzed and she clicked the button. Ted's familiar face popped up on her screen. "Hey, there beautiful," he said with a giant grin. "Aren't you a sight for sore eyes."

"I could say the same about you," she said, her lips curving up to form a happy smile. "It feels like forever since I've seen you and it hasn't even been a week."

"Well, we used to see each other every day, so a week feels like a month."

She nodded. "Did you decide what movie we're going to watch?"

He shrugged. "I figured after putting this off for the past couple of days, the least I could do was let you pick."

"Trying to butter me up, are you?" she teased, flipping her red curls over her shoulder. "You know I like it when I'm in charge."

"You know I do," he flirted back, giving her a wink.

"I guess if I get to pick, I will go with one of my favorites. I also know we can stream it from both our TVs. How about *50 First Dates.*"

A look of relief flooded Ted's face. "Whew, I

was worried you were going to pick some chick flick or drama."

She let out a laugh as she shook her head. "If I wanted you to fall asleep, I'd pick one of those. I know better than that. I figured this is the best of both worlds. It's got comedy and romance. Besides, I love Drew Barrymore."

Ted quirked one eyebrow as he tilted his head. "Is that the real reason or is it because I remind you of Adam Sandler and their relationship reminds you of ours?"

"You mean besides the fact that she has amnesia and can't remember him?"

"Well, I guess not that part. I was talking more about how he's goofy and bumbles everything, and she's gorgeous and perfect and way too good for him."

"You really are trying to butter me up, aren't you?"

"You know it's true, but if it works on getting you to forgive me for my lack of attention lately, I'll take that as an added bonus."

"All right, enough of that," she said, her cheeks warming from the compliment. "I've got my popcorn. Do you have yours?"

He nodded, lifting his bowl of the golden popped kernels. "I'm ready."

"I think we're ready then," she said, leaning back into her sofa to get comfortable.

They counted down and hit the play button at the same time. The familiar images of the movie came across the screen and they both settled into their spots, engrossed in the movie. A few times, out of habit, she reached out to grab his hand during a romantic scene. Each time, an emptiness took a hold of her when she remembered he wasn't there. Even though she wanted this date to go well, it just wasn't the same as being together in a real way.

By the end of the movie, Deanna found herself wondering how she was going to be able to handle this for weeks, possibly months on end. And for what? If Ted got the job, he wouldn't be coming back. Her life was in Clear Mountain. Where did that leave them?

Ted leaned forward, looking at her in a way that made it clear he must feel the same way. Instead of admitting it though, he simply said, "I enjoyed the movie."

"I did, too. It would have been better if we could watch together—you know, in person."

"I know, but we just need to give it time. We'll

figure out a way to make this work. I care about you, Deanna."

She nodded. "I care about you, too."

"I have to get ready for training tomorrow. I'll text you afterward."

"Sounds good. Stay safe."

As the video screen went black, her heart felt like it was filling with the same void. She didn't want to think they couldn't make it, but she wondered if all of this was pointless. Pushing that troubling thought away, she stood up and took her popcorn bowl into the kitchen. As she cleaned up, she sent up a silent prayer asking God to give her patience and understanding during this difficult time.

6

It was the final day of Ted's first week of training. Though the week had started out difficult and he had been consistently in the bottom of the pack of trainees, Ted and Titan were finally getting the hang of the new search techniques. Towards the middle of the week, they managed to work their way up towards the top. In the past couple of days, they were ranking in the top three teams, and in one instance, they even got the highest marks of the twenty-four trainee teams.

"Good boy, Titan, good boy," Ted said, handing his K9 partner a treat for finding the rescue dummy that had been wedged between two pieces of concrete.

"Nice find," Instructor Dixon praised, coming

up beside them and marking it down on his clipboard. "That's your third for this session. Soon enough, you'll be steadily out-performing all the other trainees."

"Maybe we didn't make a mistake by picking him for the potential instructor position after all," Instructor Bilmont said as he approached the pair. "I wasn't so sure at the beginning of the week, but he's turned it around."

"I don't know. He still has three weeks to go," Instructor Griffin chimed in as he joined the group. "Sometimes a trainee gets a burst of luck, and then it dwindles out. The key is to see if he can keep up the results."

"Care to make a bet on it?" Dixon asked, crossing his arms. "I bet you a night out at the bar in Woody that he makes it through to the end."

"Can I get in on this?" Bilmont interjected. "I bet he not only makes it to the end, but graduates at the top of the class."

What on earth was going on? Why did these men think it was acceptable to bet on his future? He wasn't an action figure they could toss around like he was a toy.

Griffin rolled his eyes. "All right, you're both on. You two have way too much faith in this guy. If he washes out—which I think he will—you both owe *me* a night of drinks."

"But if he graduates at the top—you owe both of us drinks for the night," Bilmont countered.

"Deal," Griffin said, shaking both men's hands.

Ted turned away, disgusted. He gently tugged on Titan's leash, making it clear he wanted to get away. Just when he thought he was doing good, they made him feel worthless again. What was wrong with these guys?

"Where do you think you're going, Trainee?" Griffin asked, his voice making it clear he wasn't dismissed.

Even though he didn't want to, Ted stopped in his tracks. He paused, inhaled deeply, then turned around, ready for the next verbal assault.

Griffin moved forward until he was only inches away from Ted. He narrowed his steely gray eyes until they were merely slits. "The other guys saw something in you, and that's why you got this spot to begin with. I want you to know, I don't see it. I think you've simply managed to find a little luck, but luck doesn't cut it in this job. You have to have gumption, determination, skill."

Ted lifted his chin up in defiance. "You don't know me then. I have all of those traits in spades.

I'm going to prove you wrong if it's the last thing I do."

Griffin looked shocked at first, then almost pleased for a moment, before it was quickly masked by a look of apathy. "Whatever, Trainee, get back to work."

Ted pushed himself even harder, wanting to show Griffin he was dead wrong about him. He was a great cop, and an even better K9 handler. By the end of the final session, Ted had managed to find three more rescue dummies, which put him two rescues above the rest of the trainees. It tied him for the best first week performance of any trainee. *Take that, Griffin.*

Apparently, word got around about his record for the week. At dinner that night, several of the other trainees came up and congratulated him on his accomplishment. What surprised him most was that Adam even came up and did the same.

"Congrats, Ted," Adam said, sitting down next to him and patting him on the back. "I knew you were going to do great here when I recommended you for the spot."

"I thought it was a rule that instructors weren't supposed to fraternize with the trainees."

"I thought you knew by now, I do what I want,

and what I want to do right now is congratulate my friend for a job well done." He stood up, and before he turned around to leave, he added, "Keep it up. I look forward to when you come out on the other side a full-fledged team member. It'll be nice to have an old friend around here."

Ted's heart filled with warmth from the acknowledgement. Even though he felt like he was alone here, he had to remind himself he had a friend in his corner. Not only that, but God was also on his side. As long as he continued to hold onto his faith and remembered God made him for this job, no one could tear him down enough to make him quit. He was going to graduate from the academy and prove everyone who doubted him wrong.

DEANNA WAS NERVOUS. It had been an impulse decision to buy the ticket to Dallas. When her work week ended and she realized she wasn't on the volunteer schedule for church, she suddenly had a free weekend at her fingertips. Wanting to see Ted was all she could think about, and she found herself booking a ticket via her phone. Three hours later, she was boarding a plane headed for Texas.

"Ladies and Gentlemen, welcome to Dallas, the jewel of the Lone Star state," the pilot's voice boomed over the intercom. "You will find the weather to be a perfect 71 degrees today with not a cloud in the sky. Enjoy your stay and fly again with us here on Allied Airways."

A few minutes later, the plane came to a stop at the terminal. The seatbelt light went out, letting the passengers know they could get up to disembark. Deanna stood up and pulled her carry-on down from the overhead compartment. She had strategically packed a small enough bag that she wouldn't have to check it. She didn't want to take the chance that her luggage got lost when she was only going to be there for a couple of days.

She picked up her rental car and entered the address for the Disaster City Search and Rescue Academy. Even though she didn't tell Ted she was coming, she hoped he wouldn't mind her surprising him with a visit. She figured it was the weekend, so he was probably resting and bored stiff. This way, at least they could spend some time together before they both got back into their work weeks.

It was a quick half hour drive to the academy, and when she arrived at the place, Deanna was surprised by how active the academy was even though it was the weekend. She pulled into one of the spots in the parking lot and climbed out. As she walked through the campus, she was surprised that everyone seemed like they were still working. She was starting to have second thoughts about bothering Ted, but before she could change her mind, someone came and tapped her on the shoulder.

"Can I help you, miss?" the young blond man asked with curiosity. "You look lost."

"Do I look that out of place?"

"Well, we only have a handful of women at the academy currently, so you stick out like a sore thumb."

"I'm here to see my boyfriend, Ted Hendricks. He's training at the academy."

"Oh, I know, Ted. We met the first day of training. I'm Kenneth Daniels," he said with a friendly smile. "He's staying on the same floor as me. I can take you to his room."

Kenneth escorted her across the rest of the campus and guided her into a large building. They climbed the stairs to the second floor and headed to the end of the hallway.

"His room is this one," Kenneth said, stopping in front of the second to the last door. "It was nice meeting you."

"It was nice meeting you, too," she said, right before he swiveled around and sauntered off back down the hall.

Deanna turned to the door and knocked. A few seconds later, she heard the pattering of little paws, followed by footsteps. The door swung open to reveal Ted and Titan on the other side.

He looked shocked to see her. He blinked several times before he stammered out, "What… what are you doing here?"

"I came for a visit," she said, giving him a smile she hoped would convince him to be happy about it.

"Why didn't you tell me you were coming?" he asked, raising his arm and running his hand through his brown hair.

"I wanted it to be a surprise." Glancing past him, she asked, "Aren't you going to invite me in?"

He stepped back, causing Titan to move further back as well. "Sure, come on in."

She entered and followed behind him. There was a living room and the further back two doors she assumed led to the bedroom and bathroom. It wasn't a huge space, but still nice.

"So, this is where you're living? It looked bigger on video."

"I don't need much," Ted said, gesturing to the couch in the living area. "Why don't you take a seat while I grab us a couple of waters."

Deanna did as he suggested. She looked around, trying to distract herself from his less than stellar welcome. In her mind, when she pictured seeing him for the first time since he left, she thought he would grab her and pull her into a huge hug. What she didn't expect was for him to seem bothered by her arrival.

Ted came back into the room and handed her a bottle of water. "Here you go." He took a seat next to her on the couch.

"You don't seem happy to see me."

"It's not that," he said, shaking his head. "I just have a lot on my plate with the academy. I was planning on studying this weekend, so I'm ready for next week's exercises for natural disaster training. I haven't had a lot of experience with earthquake searches."

"Oh, I didn't mean to distract you from what you need to do. If you need me to leave, I can do that," Deanna said, trying to hide her disappointment.

Ted let out a heavy sigh. "You came all this way. It would be a shame to send you back now." He reached out and pulled her towards him. "I'm sorry about my reaction. I am happy to see you."

It felt good to be in Ted's arms again. She had missed it. When his lips came down to meet hers, it was like putting on her favorite sweater: warm and familiar. She let herself melt into his arms, enjoying his embrace and how secure it made her feel.

She felt the wet nose of Titan nuzzle between them, breaking the moment. Deanna pulled back and laughed. "What, boy, did you miss me, too?"

He barked as if to answer her, wagging his tail.

"I'll take that as a yes. I've missed you, too," she said, reaching out and rubbing him between the ears.

"I could stay here and kiss you all day, but I have to admit, I'm starving. I haven't left the DCSRA facility since I arrived. We could go explore some, if you're up for it?"

She nodded. "I'd like that."

"Let me go throw on some jeans and a button-up," he said, gesturing to his black sweats and white t-shirt.

"That's fine. I'll just spend some time with Titan until you come back."

Ted disappeared into one of the other rooms

and Deanna turned her attention to his partner. "How have you been, boy? Do you like it here?"

He barked again, wagging his tail even more quickly. Deanna wasn't sure if she liked the fact that it seemed both of them were comfortable here. If that was the case, it would mean that Ted would be more likely to stay. She knew she shouldn't want him to be miserable, but if he was, it would mean he would return home to Clear Mountain. The longer he stayed at the academy and got used to it, the less likely it would be that he would ever leave.

"Okay, let's go," Ted said, gesturing for them to head out of the dorms.

The trio made their way to his truck, where Ted put Titan into his kennel in the back. They took off down the highway but were only on it for a few minutes before they turned onto a two-lane road.

"Where are we going?"

"Some of the instructors mentioned this nearby small town called Wilmont. It's supposed to be right out of a Hallmark movie. I know how much you love those and figured we could head over there."

"Really? That sounds amazing," Deanna said, clapping her hands together in excited anticipation. "I can't wait."

They were only on the road for about fifteen

more minutes before buildings started coming into view. There was a cute wooden sign that read, "Welcome to Wilmont, Where Everyone is Family."

As they rambled down Main Street, Deanna couldn't help but fall in love with the small town. True to the description, it looked just like a Hallmark movie with vintage brick buildings, benches and flower pots that dotted the sides of the street, and even a town square with a white gazebo. She saw a coffee shop with the name, *The Perfect Blend,* in bold letters across the top. "Stop the truck! We have to go there," she exclaimed. "I bet you they have the best coffee."

Ted found a nearby parking space along the street. They climbed out of the truck, grabbed Titan, and made their way over to the coffee shop. They entered the adorable little shop that was filled with homemade baked goods and the most delicious smell of freshly brewing coffee. A friendly barista took their order, and a few minutes later, they took their coffee and pastries to a back corner table.

Deanna handed Titan his doggie treat before settling into her chair to enjoy her own. "This place is great. I mean, I like Superior Coffee, but if we had this place in Clear Mountain, I would definitely be going there."

"It is nice," Ted conceded, "and the coffee's great."

They finished their drinks, then headed out. They walked arm-in-arm down the street with Titan beside them. There was an adorable little gift shop at the corner, called, *The Garden Shed,* which looked like it used to be an old cottage that had been converted into a storefront. Deanna decided they should go in. The shop was filled with all sorts of trinkets, including hats and scarves, wind chimes and garden signs, writing pens and notepads, pots of herbs and bottles of essential oils, plus various other odds and ends. They wove their way through the different sections, picking up items and looking at them. At the very back, there was another sign that read, *Enter our Garden.*

To Deanna's complete awe, they stepped into what could only be described as a fairytale land filled with wonder. Each area was themed after famous stories. There were several sections including Mermaid Cove, Alice's Tea Party, Hogwarts' Castle, Snow White's Cottage, Narnia, and Fairy Land with quotes written on wooden signs, figurines from the stories, and whimsical benches to sit and enjoy the experience.

"I can't believe how amazing this place is," Deanna marveled. "I feel like I'm in a dream."

"I love watching you take all of this in," Ted said with a grin. He reached out and pulled her towards him. "You look like a child opening a present for the first time. I have to say, it's really appealing."

There were strings of lights twinkling above them, and she felt his arms grab her around the waist. He dipped his head down and claimed her lips with his own. Her hands moved up and wrapped around his neck as he deepened the kiss. The moment was perfect, and Deanna couldn't be happier.

Titan's ferocious barking interrupted their kiss, pulling their attention towards him. A squirrel had darted up a nearby tree and was causing him to go crazy with excitement underneath it.

"It's okay, boy, it's just a squirrel," Ted said, pulling on his leash in an attempt to calm his K9 partner. "Just calm down." Glancing around, Ted whispered, "I think we should get out of here before we make a bigger scene."

Deanna nodded. "You ready for dinner?"

"You know me; I can always eat," he teased with a wink. "I heard that there's a great café just around the corner."

They made their way over and asked to be seated on the patio so Titan wouldn't bother anyone inside. The server came and took their order, then they were left on their own.

"This has been a really nice day," Deanna said. "Thanks for bringing me here."

"You know, once I graduate from the academy and get the permanent spot on the DCSR team, we might want to think about you moving here. Could you see yourself living in this place?"

"I don't know. I really love my life in Clear Mountain. I've never thought about moving anywhere else."

"Well, you might need to if we want to make this work," Ted pointed out. "Can you at least start thinking about the possibility of it?"

Deanna nodded. "I can do that."

"After dinner, we'll have to head back to the academy though. We have a strict eight o'clock curfew."

"I totally understand. I don't want to get you in trouble."

"Where are you staying tonight?"

"I got a room in Dallas. I knew you were staying in the dorms, and figured I'd need a place to stay."

He nodded. "What time is your flight back tomorrow?"

"I have one booked for three. I need to get back in time to get ready for work and figured you would have to get ready for your second week at the academy. I looked up churches online, and there's one I wanted to check out near my hotel. Care to join me in the morning?"

She could tell he was debating. After a moment, he nodded. "Sure, I think I can manage that. Just text me the address and time."

They finished the rest of their time in Wilmont before heading back to the academy. They said their goodbyes before Deanna left to go to the hotel. On her drive there, she wondered what it would be like if she did move here. How much would she miss her friends? Her church? Her job? Could she be happy without all those things in her life? Was Ted important enough to her to give all of it up to be with him? She didn't have any of the answers and wasn't sure when she would.

That night in bed, she found herself asking God to help her determine the path her life was supposed to be on. She wasn't sure what direction she was supposed to go, but she knew she couldn't figure it out on her own.

THE NEXT MORNING, Ted met her at the church just like he promised. It was another Assembly of God church. It was very different than the one they attended in Clear Mountain; traditional in both the style of music and attire. It wouldn't be a place she would frequent, but she did appreciate the pastor's message about hope and love.

Afterward, Ted suggested they go to lunch before she had to return her rental car and head to the airport. They found a quiet little bistro only a couple of blocks away.

They asked the hostess to seat them at a back table where they could have some privacy.

"It's been nice spending time with you," Ted admitted. "I'm going to miss you when you're gone."

"I know. I don't want to go. It stinks we both have work tomorrow."

He nodded, reaching out and squeezing her hand across the table. "I wish we had more time together."

"Let's just enjoy what we have."

They spent their last hour together enjoying their meal and talking about everyone back in Clear Mountain. Deanna asked a couple of questions about the academy and Ted's instructors. The time went by fast, and before she knew it, they were leaving the restaurant.

As they stood by their vehicles, she could tell Ted didn't want to say goodbye. He was shifting his stance from one leg to the other.

Deanna reached out and placed her hand on the side of his face. "It's okay, Ted. I know this is hard. I hate saying goodbye, too."

"I really like having you here. It's going to be hard adjusting to you being gone again."

"We just have to make the best of the current situation. It won't be forever."

Ted placed his hand on hers. "I hope not. I can't imagine my life without you in it." He pulled her in a final time, letting his lips move down to hers in a final farewell. This kiss wasn't like the rest. It was filled with sadness and regret. Neither of them wanted to say goodbye, but they knew they had to.

"Text me and let me know you got home safely," Ted said, helping her into the car. "I don't care how late it is. I want to make sure you're okay."

She nodded. "Will do. In the meantime, go study so you can make me proud."

As she drove off, she watched Ted in her rearview mirror. He was on the edge of the street with his hands pushed into his khaki pants pockets, his head hung low. His dejected figure would be the last thing she saw before he drifted out of sight. It wasn't the way she wanted to remember him, but it seemed it was all she was going to have to keep her going until she was lucky enough to see him again.

7

It had been a long weekend, and Ted was paying the price for it. He couldn't keep his focus on the task at hand and found himself searching the same areas over and over. It resulted in him finding the least amount of rescue dummies in the group.

"What is going on with you, Trainee? Was Griffin right about you? Are you going to wash out?" Dixon asked with disgust. "I thought you would at least stay in the middle of the pack, but this performance is less than dismal. I can't even look at you right now."

"I'm going to be really mad if I end up having to buy Instructor Griffin a night of drinks because you decided to play around with your girlfriend all weekend rather than study the new techniques and rest up," Bilmont said with a shake of his head.

"You know about that?" Ted asked with apprehension.

"We told you, trainee, we see everything," Griffin said with a stern voice. "Of course, we know about your little redheaded girlfriend making a surprise visit this past weekend. My colleagues think it explains why you're doing so bad today, but I think it's because your luck ran out. I think you don't have the skills to keep up with the rest of your fellow trainees, and your lack of true experience is finally shining through."

"I still think you can pull it together and turn this around," Bilmont said in an encouraging voice. "You just need to make sure you don't let your personal life get in the way of your time here at the academy. This is the most important time in your career, your life, and you can't let anything get in your way."

"Not even a smoking hot firecracker like that looker of yours," Dixon added. "She's enough to distract any man, which is why you need to make sure she's not sniffing around here anymore. Don't disappoint us, trainee."

Ted knew they were right. He hadn't wanted to

hurt Deanna's feelings and tell her it had been a mistake for her to come to the academy. The truth was though, he was paying for trying to make her happy rather than putting his career first. This wasn't the place to mess up, and he needed to stop worrying about anything other than graduating at the top of his class.

Next time he talked to Deanna he was going to have to tell her in no uncertain terms, she couldn't come see him anymore. If he let her distract him again, he might not get the position with the team. He didn't have a fallback plan. So if this didn't work out, he wasn't sure what was going to happen to him and Titan.

"I understand," Ted said to his instructors. "I won't let it happen again."

"Good; get back to work," Griffin said, gesturing towards the urban rubble setting they were searching.

Ted and Titan finished out the rest of the session with a lackluster performance. They managed to squeeze in one more rescue, but it wasn't nearly enough to even qualify as a decent day. If they kept this up, he knew they wouldn't be getting the job at the end of his training.

Afterward, Ted headed back to his dorm.

Before he made it into the building though, he saw Adam coming down the sidewalk. He didn't have a smile on his face, which made Ted wonder if he heard about Deanna's visit. If that was the case, was he angry with Ted? His friend had gone out on a limb for him and recommended him for the DCSRA position. If Ted didn't measure up, it would be a direct reflection on Adam.

Ted debated about dodging interacting with him by going in the opposite direction. Even though he could get away with it, he didn't want to do that to his friend. If Adam was upset with him, Ted would just have to take his scolding. He deserved it, after all.

"How did today go?" Adam asked with a worried look on his face.

"Not as good as I would have liked," Ted admitted.

Adam seemed to be scanning him. "You look tired."

"I am. Exhausted, actually. And before you start in on me, too, I know it was stupid to let Deanna distract me all weekend."

"I wasn't going to put it that way, exactly. I was simply going to tell you that you might want to manage your time better. If she cares about you, she should understand how important this is to you."

"I know. She just traveled all this way and wanted to surprise me. I didn't have the heart to turn her away."

"You're a good guy who cares about people, Ted. It's one of the things I like most about you. I'm going to let you in on an important secret about the academy though. This is the one place where you have to put yourself first. You have to push everything else aside and focus on your performance here. If you don't, if you let outside distractions cause you to lose focus, you will end up failing out or underperforming. You can't afford to do either one. I nearly did that to myself by being distracted by Clara. It nearly tanked my time here. I don't want you to make a similar mistake by letting your relationship with Deanna interfere with your chance to join the DCSR team."

"I know you're right, Adam. I won't let it happen again."

"Good; like I said, I want you to get that job here. I think you would be a great asset and as an added bonus, it would be nice to work together." Adam glanced down at his watch. "I have a meeting before dinner. Before I go though, let me pray with you." Adam reached out and placed his hand on Ted's shoulder. "Dear God, I ask right now that You help my friend with his situation. You can help him through it and guide him. I pray Your hand be on him and Titan. Help him to show everyone here what I already know about him; he's meant to be at DCSRA."

Ted immediately felt better after the prayer. "Thanks, Adam. I appreciate that."

"You're welcome. I'll see you at dinner in a little bit."

As Ted took off to go get changed before dinner time, he wondered how his conversation with Deanna was going to go when he told her that things were going to have to change between them if he was going to do what needed to be done to secure his position at the academy.

DEANNA HAD a long day at work. She had been tired from her trip, so when the calls stacked up in her queue, all she wanted to do was curl up into a ball and fall asleep. Unfortunately, she couldn't do that. She forced herself to handle all of the calls, finish her assistant work for the captain, and prep for the next day. By the end, she was dragging as she left the substation.

"You look awful," Janet said with a frown on her face as she glided into the office. "Maybe you should go get a facial or something."

"If I had the time, maybe I would consider it," Deanna snapped, having no patience for the annoying woman.

"You should make time. If you don't have your looks, you don't have anything in this world."

Deanna wanted to argue there were a million other things to have, like a brain, compassion, faith; however, Deanna knew all of that would be lost on her. She'd already tried to invite the other woman to church, to coffee, and even a movie with no success. She was certain it had to do with her viewing her as a threat. Deanna was not only one of the three women in the department, but also known to be the one the men tended to go after. It made Deanna direct competition for the woman who wanted all the attention for herself. It didn't matter that Deanna never wanted it, and would gladly give it up if she could.

"Besides, with your boyfriend moving several states away, you need to get ready to find yourself a new man."

"I'm not sure why you think that's going to happen. Ted and I are still together."

"Are you though? I mean, you're not actually *together* anymore. You can call it that, but I think you're both just pretending at this point." Taking her seat at the desk, Janet added dismissively, "You should go. I have a call in the queue."

Deanna was flabbergasted by the other woman's snarky comments. Was that what everyone thought about her and Ted? Did all of their friends and his family think they were just pretending they still had a relationship? All this time she thought they were making it work. Were they just fooling themselves into thinking they had a chance?

Deciding she needed Ted to reassure her that they were in this together, she called him on her Bluetooth as she drove home. He answered the phone on the third ring.

"Hello," he said, but she could tell from his voice, he wasn't in the best of moods.

"Is everything all right?"

"Not really," he stated in an irritated tone.

"What's wrong?"

"I had a really bad day at the academy today."

"I'm sorry to hear that," Deanna said in a soothing voice. What she had to discuss could wait.

She wanted to help him. "What can I do to make it better? Can I pray with you?"

"Look, Deanna, I appreciate you trying to help. The truth is, I had a bad day because I was exhausted from our weekend together, not to mention the extra time I had to spend staying up late to study after you left. It turned out to be my worst performance since arriving at the academy. My instructors chewed me out, Adam told me I wasn't doing a good job, and I feel like crap."

"I really am sorry, Ted. I had no idea my visit would cause this kind of problem."

"Well, it did. And now I have to find a way to climb out of this hole it's put me in."

Deanna's grip on her steering wheel tightened until her knuckles were turning white. "The way you're saying that, it sounds like you're blaming me for your problems at the academy."

"I know it's not fair, and I don't want to put this on you, but I have to make some changes if I want this job on the DCSR team."

Deanna inhaled sharply. Her heart was pounding, and she could feel herself sweating with dread. "Are you breaking up with me?"

There was a long pause on the other end. "No, I'm not saying that. I still care about you, Deanna, and that hasn't changed; however, I need to focus on my time here at the academy. This is my career, my dream job we're talking about. I have to make it my priority right now. Adam said if you cared about me, you would understand."

The words felt like a slap across the face. Not only because it made her feel like she didn't matter, but because it also made her feel like she was the reason he wasn't succeeding.

Deanna choked back the tears that were forming, trying to keep herself from crying. She swallowed twice before responding. "I do care about you, Ted. You know that. If you feel this is what you need, then of course I will give you the space you need."

Without waiting for a response, she quickly got off the phone. Rather than heading home, she turned her car towards the one place where she knew she could find a sympathetic ear. She arrived at Hayley's house, and found herself knocking on the door a few moments later.

"What's wrong, Deanna? You look like you've been crying?"

Deanna sniffed a couple of times, pushing the tears away with the back of her hand. "That's because I just had a hard conversation with Ted."

"Did the two of you break up?"

"Why does everyone keep assuming that?" Deanna asked with frustration. "To answer your question, no, we didn't. He just asked me to give him some space while he's in the academy. He said my visit caused him to mess up today."

"Well, that wasn't right of him to put that on you," Hayley said, crossing her arms over her pregnant belly. "He's the only one responsible for how he does while there."

Deanna wanted to agree, but part of her knew that her visit didn't help things. She had done it out of a need to see him, but she hadn't really thought about how it would affect Ted or his time at the academy. "I wish I could agree with you, but I have to admit, I was selfish by deciding to go there. I ambushed him and basically forced him to spend the weekend with me by doing it."

"Still, he can't expect you to stay in a relationship with him like this. You deserve more than being with a man who only wants you around when it's convenient for him. That's not how a relationship works. You're supposed to be there for each other during the good *and* bad times. When it's easy *and* when it's hard. He doesn't get to push you away just because it's suddenly difficult."

"I know you have a point, Hayley. I've never wanted to admit this to anyone, but I love him. I can't just end things because we're going through a rough patch."

"I can't tell you what to do. You have to make your own decisions. I can offer to pray with you though."

Hayley and Deanna spent the next half hour praying together. It didn't fix the situation, but it did give Deanna a peace that confirmed she was doing the right thing by sticking by Ted. She wasn't going to give up on love when she finally had it for the first time in her life.

8

After a week of struggling to get back on track, Ted finished out his second week climbing back to the top. Over the weekend, he spent every free moment that he wasn't asleep, going over the new techniques and procedures he was learning. By the time the third week started, Ted felt like he was ready to take back the top spot. He was glad he didn't end up as one of the quarter of trainees that had already quit the academy and returned to their jobs. Another handful were still struggling, and Ted wanted to make sure he never ended up in that position again.

"Looking good, trainee. I think you've turned a corner," Bilmont said with pride. "You might not fail me after all."

"Don't count your chickens yet, Bilmont. We're barely halfway through the training," Griffin said, coming up and bursting Ted's bubble like he always did.

"He can count all the chickens he wants, Instructor Griffin. I'm not going to fail him, or any of you, for that matter," Ted vowed.

"Keep telling yourself that, Trainee," Griffin said before turning on his heel and heading towards the other side of the rubble training grounds.

Just as they were finishing up their second session, Deputy Commander Miller showed up and pulled their instructors aside. There was an animated discussion, with them gesturing several times back at them. After a few more minutes, they came over and told the trainees to huddle up.

"It seems there was a mudslide just outside Woody. No reported fatalities yet, but there are missing people, including two children. We've been called in to assist the local police department in their search and rescue efforts," Dixon explained.

"What that means is that you will be working your first live call since starting the academy," Griffin added. "This will test all of the new skills you've learned, not to mention your stamina. We expect you to do us proud and help find all of the victims."

"You have ten minutes to grab anything you need, then report to the staging area outside the training center," Bilmont said, gesturing towards the campus.

The trainees took off with their K9 partners and headed straight to the dormitory to gather their equipment. Ted grabbed his bag that was always ready to go, then made his way back to the designated meetup location. Everyone was buzzing around, loading supplies and dogs into kennels. Once they were ready to go, the DCSRA trucks took off and headed towards Woody.

Thirty minutes later, the team arrived in the town. The police department had their own staging area near the mudslide location. Uniformed officers as well as trained volunteers were getting assignments from the chief of police. He looked up with a look of relief on his face. "Good, the DCSR team is here. We could really use your expertise help. The mud that came down from the nearby hill wouldn't have been a problem normally, but construction of a new school had disrupted the area. When the spring rains came, it took a section of the hill with it. We have six missing people, three adult males, one woman, as well as two female children. The mudslide happened a little over two hours ago, so the quicker we can find them, the better off for them."

The chief went over the assignments with Dixon, Bilmont, and Griffin. They, in turn, assigned each team to the different areas of the grid.

"We will stay here and communicate with all of you via radio. Let us know if you have a possible location on any victims, and we will send further teams in to help with the rescue," Dixon said. "Remember, you're representing DCSR out there. Make us proud by finding all of those victims."

Ted was assigned to the west side of the affected area. It was the last known location for the missing woman and two children. Though Ted had handled his fair share of search and rescue calls in Clear Mountain, this was the first time he was working with his K9 partner. Plus, there was the added pressure that he wanted to prove to his instructors he was capable of putting into practice their techniques in the field.

He gave Titan the command to search and they worked their way along the edge of the mudslide.

There were pieces of trees and large boulders scattered through the area. They also found the edge of what looked like a small building. Most of it was covered by debris now, but from what he could identify, he thought it might be a shed. A little further down from the shed, Ted saw a piece of what looked like wood-siding from a house sticking up out of the debris. He guided Titan over to the area, using the leash to keep them close, but still giving his partner enough slack to allow him to smell the spot for clues.

Titan's sniffing and snorting quickened, and his tail started to wag as they came closer to the piece of wood. As they came closer, he could see it was a roof's edge. He followed it around and found a section of the house that wasn't covered in the debris.

Titan barked a couple of times and pawed the edge of the building. Ted moved closer and started to move more of the debris away. It was a hard process, as it was sticky and clung to everything, including his gloved hands. The structure was definitely a house and he wondered if anyone could be inside. Titan continued to bark and paw at the area. "What is it, boy, what's in there? Is it the family? Do you smell them?"

Titan barked two more times, convincing Ted he needed to let Command know they'd found something. He pushed the button on his radio. "Command, this is DCSR K-9 11, I've found what looks like a house that is covered in debris from the mudslide. My partner seems to think it's worth investigating further."

"DCSR K-9 11, last known location for the family was in that house before it was covered by the slide. It's possible they could be trapped inside." There was a pause from Command, giving him a chance to move away more debris until he found a window. He leaned forward and tried to look through the glass. It was too dirty to see anything inside.

"Command, I've found an access point. Advise if I can enter the premise to continue my search."

Anxiously, he waited for command to respond. A few seconds later, Command said, "DCSR K-9 11, please advise us of your exact location before entering. We'll send four additional teams to your location to assist, along with a dig crew."

"Copy that, Command," Ted said, opening the window. He quickly gave them his location before helping Titan through the window, and then entered behind his partner. They slowly worked their way through the room, which from what Ted could tell was the attic. There were boxes everywhere, as well as furniture draped with sheets. They had to weave through all the items as they searched. As they moved further into the room, Titan barked again. There was a small, high voice that squeaked out, "Is someone there?"

A few more steps revealed something that made Ted's heart race with exhilaration. Curled up in the corner of the room was a small figure. "My name is Officer Ted Hendricks. I'm here to help you. Can you tell me your name?"

"My mommy told me not to talk to strangers."

Ted moved a little closer and was better-able to make out the details of the girl. She looked to be about eight years old, with long blonde hair that was matted and covering her face. Her blue eyes were peeking out between the strands, and she was shivering.

"Well, then I should introduce myself so I'm not a stranger. I'm a police officer, and so is my partner here, Titan," he said, gesturing to his German shepherd beside him. He bent down and pulled his backpack around so he could open it. From inside, he pulled out a foil blanket and wrapped it around the girl's shoulders. "Do you think you can tell me your name now?"

"I guess. My name's Madison."

"Can you tell me how you got up here? Are you all alone?"

The little girl nodded. "My mom screamed from downstairs for us to run to the attic because there was a bunch of mud coming down the hill. Abigail was supposed to be behind me, but when I got to the top of the stairs I realized she never made it."

That worried Ted. If the rest of the family didn't make it into the attic, where were they? Did they make it to safety before the mudslide hit this area? If they didn't, would they be switching from searching to recovery efforts?

Ted pushed the button on his radio a second time. "Command, this is DCSR K-9 11, I've found one of the missing children inside the residence in the top floor. I haven't located the adult female or the other missing child. How long before the other teams arrive?"

"Copy that, DCSR K-9 11, the other teams should be arriving in the next five minutes. Please mark your location with a flare so they know your point of entry. We're also sending medics to assist with the treatment of the victim."

Ted gave Titan a signal to stay. "I'm going to leave Titan here with you, Madison."

"No, don't go," she whimpered out, reaching out and placing her hand on his knee. "I'm so scared. I don't want to be alone."

"You won't be. Titan is a great friend. He'll stay right by your side." Ted pulled out Titan's chew toy and gave it to him. It allowed Titan to relax and know he was off-duty for the moment.

Titan moved over and placed his head in the little girl's lap, letting her nuzzle into the top of his head. Madison rubbed along his back with her hand.

"I'll be right back," Ted promised. He took off and headed back to the window. He pulled out a flare from his backpack, cracked it and placed it outside the window. Before he could turn around though and head back, two of the other DCSR teams arrived, including Mark Turano and his K9 partner, Jagger.

"Hey, Hendricks, we hear you located one of the victims," he said with appreciation.

Ted nodded. "She's inside at the other end of the room. I left her with Titan."

"Medical should be here in a minute," Grayson Stone, one of the other trainees, said as he came up next to Turano. His K9 partner, Ghost, was beside him. "Do you have a beat on where the other two victims are?"

"The girl said they were behind her but never made it up the stairs. I think that means they're trapped somewhere in the house."

"We should get in and look then," Grayson said, helping his dog through the window and then climbing in after him. Mark did the same and soon the three of them, plus their two dogs, were inside the attic.

"Is that you, Officer?" Madison asked with hesitation.

"Yes, Madison, it's me. I also have two other officers with me and their K9 partners."

"You're right," she said with a smile. "Titan is a great friend. He's made me feel a lot better."

There was a commotion behind them. The medics were coming through the window, and made their way over to take care of the little girl.

"I have to go look for your mom and sister, Madison. These people are going to take good care of you." Ted gave Titan the signal to heel. He took his chew toy, gave him a treat for being good while with Madison, and finally commanded him to search.

The teams made their way down the attic stairs to the second floor, splitting off in opposite directions. Several of the windows were broken out and mud flow had filled part of the area; however, if they moved slowly, they were able to make their way through the debris.

Ted and Titan took the south side while Turano took the north, and Stone took the east. Whoever got finished first would finish up with the west side. A few minutes into their search, another two teams arrived and took the final area.

Titan moved through the south side sniffing for the hidden smell that would lead him to the missing victims. They made it halfway through their area, when he heard Mark say over the radio, "Command, this is DCSR K-9 16. I found the second missing child. She was hiding inside a closet. She has a few bumps and scratches, but otherwise is fine."

"Copy that, DCSR K-9 16, please take the child out of the house and relocate her to the triage area."

"Will do, Command," Turano said over the radio.

As Ted reached the staircase leading to the bottom floor, he looked down to see what he could make out. From what he could tell through the darkness, the entire bottom floor looked like it had been filled with muddy debris. If the mother had gotten swept up in that, he wasn't sure she would have survived. Ted wasn't willing to give up on her though. He pulled out his flashlight and shined it down into the staircase. "Come on, Boy, let's go see what we can find."

They tried to make their way to the bottom, but by about the bottom third, it was too thick to go any further. Ted scanned the area with his flashlight, looking for any signs of life. "Hello, anyone down here?" No response. He scanned the area again. "Hello, this is Disaster City Search and Rescue, anyone down here?" he repeated.

Ted was about to turn around to leave, but Titan started barking. He was pawing at the mud to the left of the staircase, and his barking got louder.

"Is…is someone there?" a soft female voice choked out. "I hear a dog."

Titan started to wag his tail fiercely as his barking got louder.

"Yes, ma'am, I'm a search and rescue officer. My K9 partner and I are here to help you."

"Something's wrong. I can't move." A sharp cry of pain could be heard before the woman added, "Something is pressing on me."

Ted suspected she was covered by some of the debris. The good news was her head was above it, which meant she had a fighting chance if she remained calm. "Stay still, ma'am, you might injure yourself further. There's a digging crew on their way to our location right now. I'm going to stay here with you until we get you free."

"I'm really tired. I just want to go to sleep."

"No, don't do that," Ted shouted, worried she had a head injury. If she fell asleep, she might not wake back up. "Just keep talking to me."

"What do you want to talk about?" she asked, her voice sounding strained.

"How about your daughters? I met Madison. She's a great kid. Officer Turano found Abigail."

"They're both okay?"

"Yes, they're both fine thanks to you. You kept them safe by telling them to get to higher ground."

"Good, that's good." Ted could hear the relief in her voice. "If I don't make it out of here, you tell them—"

"No, ma'am, you're not going to say your good-byes. We're going to talk about what you're going to do with your daughters when you get out of here."

Just then, the dig crew announced over the radio they had arrived. They started to work on getting the mother free. Ted kept his word and stayed the whole time. It took two hours, but they were able to make a path to her and get her free. She had four cracked ribs and a broken leg and arm, but surprisingly, the medics said she didn't have any other visible injuries.

The other three male victims were also found and rescued in the surrounding areas affected by the mudslide. By the end of the night, all the victims were accounted for.

The Wilmont police chief came forward and spoke to the group of officers and volunteers that aided in the rescue effort. "We want to thank the DCSR team for coming out here and aiding in our search and rescue effort. Without your help, we might not have recovered all the victims alive."

There were claps and cheers that echoed around the group. It had been a long day, but Ted had never felt prouder than he did working his first call as a K9 handler.

"Great job, trainee," Bilmont commended him with a smile. "I knew you were going to shine."

"Thanks," he said, returning the smile. "It was all your expert training that kicked in."

"I have to admit, you did good today," Griffin conceded. "There might be a chance I end up buying the graduation drinks after all."

Once Ted was back in his room at the dorms, he knew he should get some sleep, but he was still wired from the eventful day. He clicked the icon for Deanna on his phone, wanting to tell her the good news.

She answered on the third ring. "Hello." Her tone made it clear she was busy, but she didn't say anything else.

"I was just calling to tell you I had my first call-out as a K9 handler today. It went good, really good as a matter of fact."

"That's good, Ted. It sounds like you're really happy there." She let out a heavy sigh. "Right now isn't the best time for me to talk. I have a lot of work I need to get done for the captain, and Janet called in sick today."

"Oh, I'm sorry. She really hasn't been pulling her weight."

"She's not the only one," Deanna snapped out. "Look, I have to go. I'll talk to you later." She didn't wait for a response, but instead hung up.

Ted wasn't sure what he expected when he called Deanna, but how she just reacted wasn't it at all. It took the wind right out of his sails. Even though he had told her he needed space while he was going through the academy, he didn't mean he wanted complete radio silence. Over the past week and a half though, he'd noticed that she hadn't been responding to or sending as many texts as she had previously. She also let several of his calls go to voicemail or cut the phone call short when she occasionally did answer.

He hadn't meant to hurt Deanna, but it seemed that was what happened. He wondered if it was only a matter of time before she broke up with him.

THE MOMENT she hung up on Ted, she regretted it. The truth was, she was still hurt from the conversation they had about him needing space. Add in that she had a difficult week covering for Janet along with extra work required by the captain, and Deanna felt like she was drowning in trouble.

The only good thing was tonight she had Bible study. She always felt better when she went and spent time with her friends in the Word of God.

Deanna made it home just in time to change out of her work clothes and into a pair of jeans and a green blouse. She pulled her hair up in a quick ponytail, grabbed the cake she was taking, then climbed back into her car to head over to Lindsay's house.

A few minutes later, she arrived. She knew she could just head inside, so she entered through the front door.

Brooke was the first to greet her. "Hey there, friend, how you hanging in?"

Deanna shrugged. "Better now that I'm here. I swear Janet is going to be the death of me."

"I know she's tough to deal with, but you've got this," Erica encouraged with a friendly smile.

"Am I the last to arrive?" Deanna inquired.

"I'm not sure Hayley is going to make it," Lindsay said, taking the cake and adding it to the other food on the kitchen counter. "She called earlier today and told me she was having contractions."

Deanna's eyes grew wide with worry. Did that mean her best friend was going to have her baby tonight?

Lindsay must have recognized Deanna's reaction, because she quickly explained to the group,

"Don't worry, she's doing fine. She just needs to rest. The doctor said she could have a couple of days of contractions before she would need to go to the hospital."

The women went into the living room and took seats in the chairs and on the couch. They pulled out their Bibles and study plan.

"Before we get started, does anyone have any prayer requests?" Lindsay asked.

The other women listed sick relatives, work problems, and of course, Hayley. Deanna debated whether she should bring up what happened with Ted. Deciding she could use the support and prayer, she opened up.

"I had a fight with Ted today. He called to tell me about something great that happened to him at the academy, but I wasn't supportive. Actually, it was worse than that. I was mean and condescending about it. He didn't deserve it, but I was still so hurt from when he told me he needed space. I could really use some prayer for the situation."

"That's what we're here for, to support each other," Erica said, reaching out and patting her arm. "Relationships can be tough, especially when you're dating a cop. It's hard to balance the job and a personal life. You just need to have patience. It's clear how much Ted cares about you."

"Thanks, guys, I appreciate it."

The group spent the next fifteen minutes praying over all the requests. By the end, Deanna felt a peace enter her heart.

"Do you guys mind if I step out and call Ted really quick?"

"No, of course not. We can all grab some snacks while you do that," Lindsay said.

Deanna made her way out onto the front porch. She clicked the number next to Ted's picture. It rang several times, but he didn't answer. She decided to leave him a message. "I'm sorry about earlier, Ted. I could give you a bunch of excuses, but the truth is, you didn't deserve how I treated you. I'm going to do better. I promise. Call me when you can."

Even though she didn't get to talk to him, she felt better about the situation. At least she could rest in the fact she apologized and told him she would keep from doing it in the future.

Deanna entered the house and found the women rushing around in a frenzy.

"What's going on?"

"Connor just called the house. Hayley's at the

hospital and about to give birth to the baby," Lindsay explained.

"We all want to go down there and support them," Brooke added. "You coming?"

Deanna nodded. "Let's go."

A half hour later, the group of friends arrived at the hospital and made their way up to the labor and delivery wing. They found their husbands and boyfriend sitting in the waiting room.

"You guys made it just in time," Aiden said with a grin. "Hayley just had the baby."

"When can we see them?" Deanna asked, ecstatic to hold her first niece.

"The nurse told us she could have two visitors at a time in an hour," Zach explained. "She needs to rest for a bit."

When the time was up, Deanna was one of the first to go in the room. Brooke was with her. Hayley was sitting up in her hospital bed, holding Addie Marie in her arms. She was pink, chubby, and perfect.

"She's adorable," Deanna cooed as she approached them. "I can't believe you're a mom now."

"Right? It still doesn't feel real," Hayley said

with a smile. "I had no idea I could love somebody this much when I just met them."

"It's pretty amazing," Connor agreed from his spot in the chair next to her.

"You want to hold your new niece?" Hayley offered.

"Are you sure?"

Hayley nodded. "You're family."

Deanna reached out and took the baby into her arms. She was careful to support her neck and head as she pulled her in close, letting the tiny bundle fill her with awe. "She's so light," Deanna mused. "I had no idea she would be as weightless as a feather."

"She won't be for long," the nurse said, coming into the room. "They grow like weeds."

Connor chuckled. "If she's anything like me, she sure will. My mom said I nearly ate her out of house and home."

"You were a boy; girls don't do that," Hayley said with disdain.

"Oh, I don't know about that. I've seen plenty of girls that have a healthy appetite," the nurse said, as she hung the new IV bag.

By the time Deanna was ready to let a couple of the other women come and see the baby, she realized that what she wanted most out of life was a family, and she wanted that family with Ted. Once he was finished with the academy, she was going to tell him that she was willing to move to Texas to be with him. It might mean giving up her life in Clear Mountain, but Ted was worth it.

9

The final week of training was wrapping up, and Ted was at the top of his class. After finding the missing family during the mudslide, Ted continued to excel during the rest of the exercises. He'd already broken two records and was close to breaking a third.

As good as things were going with his career, the same couldn't be said for his personal life. He couldn't manage to catch a break with Deanna. They both kept missing each other's phone calls, texts were sporadic at best, and neither of them seemed to have time for video chatting. He cared about her, but it seemed every time he tried to fix things with her, something got in the way.

There was a knock at the door, causing Ted to

walk over and open it. Adam was standing on the other side. "Can I come in?" he asked.

"Sure," Ted said, stepping back to let him enter. "I know the rules about you hanging out with a trainee. Are you here to give me a head's up? Did I do something that's going to get me into trouble?"

Adam shook his head, "No, just the opposite. I'm actually here to congratulate you on how great you are doing. I know training isn't officially over yet, but I wanted to tell you, the disaster instructors are impressed with you. Dixon said he hasn't seen as much raw talent in a handler as you in years. Bilmont thinks you might be the best one in a generation. Griffin—well, he's Griffin and won't give an inch—but I can tell he's happy with your performance, too. They told me unofficially, you're getting the opening in their department."

"Really?" Ted's eyebrows shot up in surprise. "I mean, I knew that that was the goal when I came here, but to hear it's actually happening feels incredible."

"I wanted to be the one to tell you, but you should still act surprised when you get the official offer." Adam went over and sat down on the couch, picking up the remote for the TV. "Since you're going to be on staff here soon, I figured there wasn't any reason we couldn't hang out now. Care to watch the game together?"

"I should really study for the last exam, but I guess I can take a break." Ted joined his friend on the couch and settled down to watch the basketball game. It was nice to have a friend again, but it didn't keep his mind from drifting back to Deanna every now and then. He really needed to figure out a way to make it work with her. He cared about her, and he didn't want to lose her.

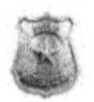

THE NEXT FEW days flew by, and graduation was approaching. Soon, Ted would be receiving his certificate from the academy, then he would get his very own shining Disaster City Search and Rescue badge. He couldn't wait until the Commander handed it to him and he could add it to his blue cargo uniform.

Today was the final exercise before graduation. The trainee that achieved the most rescues during the live simulation would be able to finish the academy with the recognition that they were truly the best of the best. Ted wanted that honor.

Ted stepped into the rubble-filled training

grounds. He couldn't believe how much detail they put into the simulation. There were several wrecked cars, a bus, and an airplane, not to mention building façades that were falling down and chunks of concrete and debris all over the sidewalk and road. Added with the live victims, volunteers, and medical staff that would help make the scenario come to life, it would feel exactly like a real-life urban disaster.

As the teams were released into the area, Ted made his way straight for the plane crash. He had a hunch that there would be several victims in the area. It wouldn't take much to pick through it, and he and Titan could get several rescues under their belt quickly. Ted's instincts were correct. Within a few minutes, Titan found their first victim sandwiched between two passenger seats towards the back of the plane. He gave Titan room to work. His K9 partner led him farther up and under another seat mid-way through the plane where he found a second victim. That made two in less than twenty minutes. It was a good start, but he wanted to see if he could get three in thirty.

They finished searching the rest of the plane, and Ted was about to have them leave the area when Titan started to bark and wag his tail near an airplane that was on the ground. Ted followed as Titan got closer. The edge of a tennis shoe could be seen sticking out. Ted bent down and found his third victim just before the thirty-minute mark. That had to be a record.

Not stopping to find out, he left the airplane area and made his way towards one of the building façades. Just like before, Ted let Titan have enough room to do his job.

By the end of the final two-hour exercise, Ted and Titan had found seven victims. The rest of his team and the instructors were congratulating them on setting a new academy record. The praise and accolades felt good. It was a confirmation that Ted was doing what he was always meant to do.

They were wrapping up and getting ready to head back to the dorms before dinner when the deputy commander came rushing up to the team. He had a worried look on his face as he pulled their instructors aside.

A few minutes later, Griffin came forward and addressed the group. "Trainees, there has been a natural disaster that we've been asked to help assist with search and rescue. The city of Boulder, Colorado, experienced a 6.5 magnitude earthquake an hour ago. There has been major damage to the area. Hundreds, possibly thousands, of people are trapped inside dilapidated buildings and vehicles. We'll be heading there in fifteen minutes via our fleet of helicopters. You are to go grab whatever gear you and your K9 partner need and meet at the staging area to prepare for departure. This is what we are trained for. You will be in the most intense, extreme search and rescue conditions possible. Prepare yourself to enter a devastated area."

The trainees took off for the dorms, but before Ted could leave the area, Bilmont reached out and stopped him. "Aren't you from that area, Hendricks?"

"Yes, I am. I have a lot of friends that live in Boulder, but that just makes me want to do my job even more."

"Are you sure? You don't want to sit this one out?" Dixon offered.

Griffin came up and placed his hand on Hendricks' shoulder. "He's got this, don't you, Hendricks?" Griffin asked, but in a way that made it clear he had confidence Ted wouldn't let them down.

Ted nodded. "I'm fine. I can handle this. I want to do everything I can to help the people there."

"All right, then go gear up," Dixon said, gesturing with his head towards the dorms.

Ted took off. The first thing he wanted to do was call Deanna and see if she had any information about the earthquake. He doubted Clear Mountain was hugely affected by the earthquake. As the town was situated a half hour away, they would be assisting in rescue efforts. She would know exactly how bad it was, which would give him a better frame of mind.

The phone rang four times, then went to voicemail. Not surprising since they were in the middle of a crisis. He quickly left her a message, then hung up and texted her. Even if she was on a dispatch call, she would respond to the text. Nothing. He sent another text message, adding 9-1-1 at the end to let her know he really needed to talk to her. Still nothing. Now, he was beginning to worry. Was there a possibility that Clear Mountain had major damage? He quickly called his parents. His mother answered the phone after the second ring. From her tone, he immediately knew something was wrong.

"What is it, Mom? What's going on?"

"Have you talked to Deanna in the last couple of hours?" she asked in a pensive tone.

"No, why?"

"She decided to take Maggie to the Boulder Zoo today for her birthday. She sent me a picture from there about three hours ago, but I haven't been able to get a hold of her since the earthquake. Do you think they made it out before....?" His mother didn't finish her sentence. He could hear her choking back the tears. His mother was strong, but when it came to her family, she was like putty.

"It's okay, Mom. Deanna is smart. If they were there, she would know how to keep them both safe."

"Oh, Teddy, if something happened to either of them, I don't know what I'd do."

"It's going to be okay, Mom. I promise. How is everything in Clear Mountain? Are you and Dad safe?"

"We're fine; only minor aftershocks. The most that happened over here were a few shattered windows and broken household items. It's Deanna and Maggie I'm worried about. They were right in the center of it."

"I know. I'm worried about them, too. I'm going to call one of my friends over at Clear Mountain Search and Rescue and see what they can tell me."

Aiden picked up on the second ring, but he sounded distracted. "Hello."

"Hey, Aiden, I know you're busy with the rescue efforts over in Boulder, but I need to find out what you know. Deanna might have been at the Boulder Zoo with my niece when the earthquake hit."

"Lindsay told me that Deanna was going to surprise your niece with a trip to the zoo for her birthday. When the earthquake hit, Lindsay tried to get a hold of her without any luck. Since then, we've all tried but no one has heard from her since a few hours ago."

Ted's heart seized in his chest. Where were they? Were they okay? Did they make it out of Boulder before the earthquake happened, or were they trapped in some building, or on a remote road where no one was able to find them? What if they were hurt and no one could get to them? He had to know what he was dealing with.

"Are you guys already there? How bad is it?"

"I'm not going to sugar-coat it, Ted. The quake hit in the center of downtown, and spread from there. Between the people trying to get out and the damage, the roads are impassible. We can't get into the inner part of the city, so we're helping on the outskirts. If I could, I would try to get to the zoo myself to look for Deanna and your niece. You know how much we all care for them both, but I can't leave my team. The captain wants us to help where we're at."

"I understand, Aiden. The good news is that DCSR is being deployed to the area. We'll be going in via helicopter, so we'll be dropped near the epicenter."

"I'll be praying you find them both safe and sound. I'll text Lindsay, too, so she can have the church prayer group do the same."

"Thanks, Aiden. I really appreciate it. Stay safe."

"You, too."

As Ted ended the phone call, he wondered how bad the damage was. Earthquakes never happened in Colorado, which meant that structures weren't built to withstand the type of stress they caused. If Deanna and Maggie were near any of the buildings that came down, they could be hurt, or worse.

Ted pushed the thought from his mind. He couldn't think like that. He needed to focus on what he could do, meaning getting to her last known location quickly to perform the best search and rescue of his life.

What on earth was that noise? Deanna thought as she shook her head back and forth. Whatever it was, it wouldn't stop ringing. She tried to take in a deep breath, but she felt herself cough instead. Something was choking her every time she tried to take in a breath. She coughed three more times. *Dust, heavy, thick dust is filling my lungs. Why is it so dirty in here? Better question, where am I?*

Deanna couldn't remember where she was or how she got there. She opened her eyes and tried to look around, but everything was dark. *My phone. I have a flashlight on my phone.* She made an attempt to reach out to search for her purse, but she was boxed in by something on all sides. She barely had a few inches around her in each direction. Did she even have her purse with her? Maybe her phone was on her. She patted herself down, and to her relief, found her phone in her jeans pocket.

She touched the screen and it lit up to show Ted's face on it. *Ted. I wish he was here with me right now. Where am I, anyway? I can't remember.* Deanna racked her brain, trying to recall where she was and what happened to her. She clicked the flashlight icon on her phone and scanned the area.

From what she could make out around her, there were chunks of concrete, wires, and glass everywhere. She couldn't see anything that made sense. Nothing looked right. *What happened?*

There was a small whimper from nearby. Deanna flicked her wrist in the direction, hoping the flashlight would reveal she wasn't alone. "Is anyone there?" she choked out, but she wasn't even sure if it was loud enough for anyone to hear.

It didn't matter. She couldn't see anything. No one responded. Maybe, she imagined the whimper, anyway. Maybe, she made it herself. She wasn't sure what was going on.

There was a sudden tremor beneath her. Everything started to shake again. Suddenly, the memory of what happened came flooding back. *An earthquake, that's what happened. I was at the zoo with... Maggie! Where's Maggie?* Deanna started frantically moving her flashlight around, hoping to find the little girl she considered to be her own niece. She had been standing right next to Deanna, looking at the snakes in the reptile house.

Snakes...reptile house...if any of them got free during the earthquake, they could be anywhere by now. Deanna started twisting around, freaking out at the thought of the creatures crawling all over her. After several seconds of panic, she forced herself to calm down. She needed to get it together for Maggie's sake. Deanna took two deep breaths, then rolled over onto her stomach and started to scoot forward. "Maggie? Maggie, where are you? If you can hear me, call out to me."

No answer, but she wasn't giving up. She continued to scoot further along, hoping she wouldn't run out of room *or* run into anything that was slimy.

"Maggie, Maggie, please answer me," Deanna pleaded.

There was another whimper; this time closer than before.

"Maggie, is that you?"

"Deanna?" she heard the little girl ask in a frightened voice.

"Yes, sweetie, it's me. Where are you? Can you call out to me?"

"I'm over here," Maggie whispered a little bit louder. It sounded as if the little girl was to the left of her.

Deanna continued to move forward and, when she finally felt some space to the left, she turned. She inched her way another couple of feet, and to her relief, felt the bottom of a shoe. "Is that you, Maggie?"

"Uh-huh," she said, the tremor in her voice clear now. "I'm so scared, Deanna. Everything keeps shaking. I can't see anything. And I keep hearing…that."

There was a hissing noise coming from the other side of the concrete right next to them. Deanna quickly flashed her light at the area. Luckily, nothing was there, but it didn't mean it would stay that way.

"I think it might be safer over where I was, Maggie. Let's crawl over there."

Deanna had the little girl go first, then followed behind her. Once they were safely back in the area that Deanna hoped would remain snake-free, she thought about what they should do next.

"Let me try to call someone," Deanna said, hoping her phone call would go through. It was a long shot, considering most, if not all, the cell towers were probably down.

She dialed 9-1-1. It immediately went to a busy tone. She tried twice more, with the same result. Either it was out of order due to the earthquake, or the circuit board at the call center was overloaded. Either way, she wasn't getting through to them any time soon. Next, she dialed the Clear Mountain substation, but she got the same results. Who else could she call? Ted was in Texas, but at least he could get a hold of someone to help them. She clicked his number and it didn't go through either. She tried again with the same result. She debated trying a third time, but figured she had nothing to lose. To her relieved surprise, this time the call went through.

He answered the call right away. "Deanna, is that you?"

"Yes, Ted, it's me. I don't know how long this call will last. The reception isn't good, and my battery's running low."

"How are you? Is Maggie with you?"

"Yes, we're together. We both got banged up, but I think we're okay as far as I can tell. My head hurts a little, and I have a ringing in my ears that won't go away."

"Me, too," Maggie whispered, wrapping her arm around Deanna's waist. "And it's hard to breathe."

"She's right, Ted. It's hard to breathe in here."

"Where are you?"

"We're at the Boulder Zoo. We got trapped in the reptile house. Ted, it's a mess in here. I barely found Maggie. I'm not sure how anyone is going to find us in here."

"My team should be arriving in the next few minutes. I asked them if we could start at the zoo. They agreed. I'm going to find you both, Deanna. I promise you. No matter what it takes, I'm going to find you and bring you both home safe."

"That sounds good. I think I'll rest until you get here," Deanna said, the need to sleep starting to make her eyelids feel heavy.

"No, don't do that, Deanna. You and Maggie need to stay awake. I think you both might have concussions. If that's the case, you can't fall asleep. Talk to each other; keep each other awake."

"Okay, we'll do that," Deanna promised, forcing herself to stay alert. "Just hurry, Ted. Between the loose snakes in the area, the air that's getting dirtier by the minute, and the building continuing to shake, I'm not sure how long we can last."

10

With nowhere for the helicopters to land, the twenty-one teams combined from missing persons and disaster relief repelled down via ropes with their K9s strapped to their chests. Once on the ground, Ted and Titan took off for the reptile house. He had already looked it up on the map while they were en route, and knew the quickest way there. It wasn't easy, and Ted had to continually remind himself to remain calm, and to not push himself or Titan too fast. Rushing could get them both hurt or killed.

"Wait for us, Hendricks," he heard Griffin say from behind him. His three instructors came rushing up, along with Mark Turano and several other of his teammates. "We want to help you find your girlfriend and niece."

"Thanks, I could use the help."

"We're family at DCSRA, which means they're family," Bilmont said. "We take care of our family."

A half hour after their arrival, they reached the reptile house. Deanna had said it was a mess, but that was an understatement. If he didn't know from his map on his phone it was supposed to be there, Ted would have thought it was a pile of rubble. It looked like a bomb had hit it. He couldn't even find a door to enter.

Maybe Deanna could guide him to where they were. He dialed Deanna's number, but this time it didn't go through. It was a busy tone.

"Let's spread out and search the area," Dixon suggested. "You two and Bilmont head to the north," he pointed to some of the trainees. "Burdue and I will take the east, Griffin and you two can take the west, and Hendricks and Turano can take the south."

The teams took off in their designated search areas. They worked their way through the rubble, letting their dogs sniff anything that might help them locate Deanna and Maggie. It was a slow process, and there were even a couple of close calls with some reptiles that had escaped their cages. Ted wasn't sure if any of them were poisonous, but he wasn't about to get close enough to find out. He just hoped Deanna and Maggie were able to steer clear of them, as well.

"MAGGIE, don't fall asleep. You need to tell me what you want to do when we get out of here."

"I want to go home," the little girl whined. "It's so cold in here. I don't like the cold."

"I know, Maggie. I don't like it, either, but your uncle is coming. He's going to find us, and soon we'll be nice and cozy by a warm fire."

"That sounds nice," Maggie sighed with contentment. She curled up against Deanna. "I like to fall asleep by the fire."

"No, Maggie, you can't fall asleep," Deanna lightly scolded, shaking the little girl to keep her alert. "Your uncle said we can't fall asleep."

"He's bossy," Maggie said in a way that made it clear she didn't like it. "But I still love Uncle Teddy."

"I know. I do, too."

Maggie started squirming, moving her legs back and forth.

"What's wrong, Maggie?"

"I don't know. I feel like something's in my boot."

"What do you mean, there's something in your boot? Do you mean like a rock?" Deanna asked, hoping that was the case rather than the possibility that something slithered inside.

"I don't think so. It's moving," she whimpered. "Get it out, Deanna, get it out! There's a snake in my boot!"

Deanna reached down and grabbed the little girl's shoes. She yanked them off, and something wet and gooey came tumbling out. Deanna shrieked as it scurried up her body, stopped just at her face, and licked her. She clicked on her flashlight, petrified of what she would find. To her utter shock, it wasn't a snake at all, but just a small, green lizard. As soon as the light hit the creature's eyes, it took off running in the other direction.

Deanna let out a heavy sigh of relief. "It was just a lizard."

"This time," Maggie cried out. "What if a snake finds us? I heard them hissing earlier."

"Ted will get to us before a snake does,"

Deanna said, trying to sound optimistic. "It's going to be okay."

Some time had passed, and Deanna wasn't sure how much. She was trying to save what little battery she had left. It was hard to stay awake, but she was managing to do it. The more time passed though, the harder it was to convince Maggie to do the same. If it wasn't for Maggie, she might have given in to sleep and was considering it when she thought she heard something.

"Deanna, are you here? Maggie, can you hear me?" the familiar voice of Ted called out.

"Yes, yes, we're here," Deanna croaked out.

"Deanna, Maggie, answer me if you can," Ted continued.

"We're right here," Deanna yelled as best she could.

"Uncle Teddy, come help us," Maggie cried quietly.

"Maggie, Deanna, say something," Ted pleaded.

"I don't think he can hear us," Deanna lamented. "I think the rubble's too thick and we're too far beneath it. All this dirt in the air is making it impossible for us to shout loud enough." Deanna felt around for anything she could use to help them. Her hand came across a piece of metal. It felt like a pipe. She picked it up and started pounding on another piece of metal. She continued over and over, hoping he would hear it.

Just as she was about to give up, she heard Ted say, "I think I hear someone pounding on something below. It sounds like it's coming from down there."

There was movement above them; pieces of rubble and debris were being shifted around. Light started to come through the cracks of the concrete walls, and to her sheer relief, she saw Ted's face come into view. He was surrounded by several other men in blue uniforms.

"It's them. I can see them both," Ted shouted in excitement. "We've found them."

They continued to remove enough rubble until they were able to get to Deanna and Maggie. They came down into the area, checked them out to make sure they were safe to move, then helped them out of the hole.

"Thank you," Deanna said, folding her arms around Ted's neck. "I don't know what we would've done if you hadn't come to rescue us."

"Thank you, Uncle Teddy," Maggie said, wrapping her arms around his waist. "I knew you would save us."

He draped his arms around both of them, hugging them back.

Titan barked, wagging his tail.

"You, too, Titan, you're such a good, boy," Maggie said, rubbing the dog between his ears.

There was a hissing sound behind them, and they all jerked around to find a coiled up snake just a few feet away from them.

"Stand still," Ted said in a whisper. "If you move it's going to strike out at us."

Maggie screamed in fear. The noise must have upset the snake because it uncoiled, ready to strike. Before it could though, Titan jumped in front of it. The snake's teeth sunk into Titan's neck.

One of the other search and rescue officers picked up a metal pipe and hit the snake, killing it. The damage was done; however, Titan was bitten. He was laying on the ground, whimpering in pain.

Ted fell to his knees beside his partner. "Oh no, boy, just hold on. It's going to be okay. You did good, really good."

Deanna couldn't believe what just happened.

One moment they were celebrating their rescue, the next, Titan was attacked by a snake.

"Titan can't die, he just can't," Maggie cried. "He's such a good dog."

A frenzy of activity happened next. Ted scooped up the remains of the snake so they could identify what type it was. A DCSR helicopter arrived to evacuate them. It sent down a rescue basket for Deanna and Maggie, as well as Titan and Ted.

In the helicopter, there was the DCSR veterinarian, who traveled with the team when they were on deployment. He took a look at the reptile and assured everyone that it was a harmless garter snake.

"Titan is going to be fine. He'll be sore for a while, but he should be back to his normal self in a couple of days," the doctor assured them. "He's one lucky dog."

They arrived at the hospital in Clear Mountain where Deanna and Maggie were checked out. Though they were both fine and only had minor injuries, the doctors wanted to keep them overnight for observation. Ted's family finally arrived, hugging them with tears of relief.

Ted never left Deanna's side, but she realized there was still a state of emergency going on. "Shouldn't you be in Boulder searching for missing people?"

"I'm not leaving your side, Deanna. I nearly lost you once, I'm not taking another chance. I love you. I should have said it a long time ago, but I didn't know if we were going to make it. Now, I know, all that matters is that we're together. I'm going to give up my position at DCSRA and come back to Clear Mountain to be with you."

Deanna shook her head. "I won't let you do that. You were born to be a K9 handler. I won't let you give up your dream for me."

"You're my dream, too. I was born to love you. I'm willing to give it all up just to be with you."

"I have a better idea. You know it's always been my dream to be a police officer. I've been looking into police academies and applied for a spot in Dallas. I just got my acceptance letter on Monday. I was going to tell you at your graduation."

"You did? Does that mean you're moving to Texas?"

She nodded. "At the end of the month. I already rented an apartment online just a couple of blocks away from the Dallas academy. We'll only be a half hour apart."

"I'm so happy to hear that," Ted said, reaching out and placing a kiss on her lips. "I love you, Deanna."

"I love you, too."

11

Graduation day had arrived. Ted was standing with his fellow trainees, ready to receive their certifications of completion. Ted and Titan were graduating with the most rescues of all the trainees. On top of that, they broke six records, and Titan received an award for his heroic valor when he jumped in front of the snake to save Maggie.

As each of the names were called, Ted got more anxious. He'd already received his official job offer from DCSRA and accepted it, but this was the final piece of the puzzle he'd been putting together since he first became a cop.

"Ted Hendricks," the commander called out. Ted marched forward and accepted the certificate.

He posed for a picture, first with the commander and then with the deputy commander.

He took his seat back in the rows of classmates, pride filling his heart at a job well done.

Ted Hendricks, K9 Search and Rescue Handler
Disaster City Search and Rescue Graduate

It was a beautiful sight to behold, but as his eyes lifted up and he saw Deanna in the crowd, he realized there was something even more beautiful in this world. He was lucky enough to call her his girlfriend.

After the ceremony, Ted's family came up and congratulated him. His mother cried, his father patted him on the back, and his brothers playfully mocked him.

"Uncle Teddy, does this mean you're going to live in Texas now?"

He nodded. "My new job is here, but I promise I will come back to visit whenever I can."

"You'll bring Deanna with you, too, right? I'm going to miss you both so much."

"Of course I'll come with him," Deanna

promised, wrapping her arm through Ted's. "We're a package deal now."

"I have something to show you," Deanna said, pulling out an electronic tablet from her purse. She clicked a button and all their friends from Clear Mountain appeared on the screen.

"Congratulations!" they all shouted at once.

"We're proud of you," Aiden said with a big grin. "We knew you could do it."

"Tell Adam 'hi' for us," Zach chimed in.

"You can tell me yourself," Adam said, coming up behind Ted and peeking over his shoulder.

The group spent the next few minutes chatting about everything, including the recovery in Boulder. It was a slow process, but they were making progress every day.

When the video chat ended, the next set of people to come up to them was Ted's former instructors, who were now brand-new co-workers.

"I told you he would do it, Griffin. You owe us drinks," Dixon said with a nod of approval to Ted.

"I should get double drinks since I said he was going to graduate at the top of the class, which he did," Bilmont pointed out.

"You're both right. I owe you drinks. I also think we should bring the new guy with us," Griffin said.

"It will be a great way to get his feet wet with us as colleagues."

"I think that's a great idea," Bilmont said, nodding his head in approval. "Let's go figure out what we plan to order, Dixon."

Griffin leaned over and whispered, "Just for the record, I did it to motivate you. I knew you were going to get the position on our team the whole time. You needed the extra push, and it did just that. It made you soar."

Ted hadn't realized it, but Griffin was right. He might never have done as well if he hadn't felt the need to prove Griffin wrong. "Thanks, it seems you knew exactly what I needed."

"The best instructors always do. We'll come get you later tonight to go out."

Griffin sauntered off, leaving Ted and Deanna alone.

"Those guys are characters."

"They sure are," Ted said with a shake of his head. "They're going to keep me on my toes."

"Does that mean they're going to take my place?" she asked with a raised eyebrow.

"Nope, never. No one will ever take your place, Deanna. You're it for me."

"That goes both ways," she said, letting him

pull her into his arms. He leaned down and placed a kiss on her lips.

No matter what was to come, Ted knew two things for certain. He'd found his calling and purpose through the Disaster City Search and Rescue Academy, and gained the certainty that he wanted to spend the rest of his life loving Deanna Harper.

SNEAK PEEK OF THE BILLIONAIRE RESCUE

Christian Perez stood sternly in front of the group of fire search and rescue trainees that had made it to the final days of training. He was impressed that so many had successfully made it through the intense eight-week course at the Disaster City Search and Rescue Academy.

The eleven men and three women stood in a row at attention, exhaustion clearly written across their faces, etched in the heavy layer of grime, soot, and dirt that covered them from the rubble testing grounds. Their K9 partners sat proudly by their sides; ready for their next assignment. As their final assessment, Christian, along with his fellow fire instructors, had put their teams through a massive fire simulation that was tied to a mock arson investigation. Though all of them had passed, it hadn't been an easy test by any means. The flames were real, along with the ignitable liquids used to set them. There had also been various decoy accelerants used to throw off the dogs, as well as fake dead bodies and live victims scattered amongst the debris.

"All of you have beaten the odds. You've been tested through the rigorous process and your true grit has been proven," Christian praised. "A third of your fellow trainees quit or washed out, but those of you that remain have shown that you are the best of the best. Today, on these training grounds, you've put out the worst type of fire and cracked the hardest type of arson case. For this reason, it is my pleasure to announce that all of you will be graduating from the academy."

The trainees' tired expressions shifted to ones of pleasure as they patted each other on the back and congratulated one another. Once they settled down, Kristi Kimiko addressed the group next. "Tomorrow, you will join the most elite, most prestigious group of first responders in the country. Firefighters who can proclaim to the world that they are DCSRA graduates."

"Tonight, go out and celebrate; you've worked

hard to earn the right," Derik Cruise announced to the group.

"But don't overdo it," Christian added quickly, giving his fellow instructor a disapproving look. "Graduation is at 10 AM sharp." Then, turning back to the trainees, he added as he gestured towards the exit. "Dismissed."

The trainees, along with their K9 partners, filed out of the area, leaving Christian with Derik and Kristi.

"Do you always have to be a stick in the mud when it comes to work, Christian?" Derik asked with an irritated look. "You're one of the coolest guys I know when we're outside Disaster City, but the moment you put that blue uniform on, you instantly become a robot."

"Being professional, and expecting the same out of everyone around me, doesn't make me a robot, Derik. Just because you have an easy-breezy attitude towards everything in your life, doesn't make me a stick in the mud."

Derik shrugged, running his hands through his brown hair. "I guess I should be used to it by now, considering we've worked together for over two years. I just wish my friend showed up to work sometimes."

"Okay you two, cut it out. Don't make me break this up," Kristi sighed from the side. "We've got a lot to do before graduation tomorrow."

"Hey, I didn't start it," Christian protested, "Derik's to blame."

"Some would say it was your *winning* personality," Derik countered sarcastically with a roll of his eyes.

"Sometimes I feel like I'm your guys' mother rather than your co-worker," Kristi said with irritation. "Good thing I love my job so much, or I'd be tempted to leave without a second thought."

The men stopped glaring at each other as they turned to face Kristi.

"You wouldn't really do that, would you, Kristi?" Derik asked with a hurt tone. "We're not that bad."

"We can work on it, honestly we can," Christian added in a plea. "You know how much we need you on the team."

"Come on, let's get out of here," she said with a small laugh. "I've got somewhere to be."

The fire instructors made their way out of the training grounds and hopped into the waiting black SUV. They drove the short distance to the DCSRA veterinarian hospital where they dropped their K9 partners off for their end of assignment check-ups. Next, they made their way to the staff villa where the group parted ways.

"I've got to meet up with Aspen," Derik explained as he jumped out of the vehicle and glanced at his watch. "She's probably already waiting at the restaurant."

"I've got to go, too," Kristi said as she climbed from the back of the SUV. "Axel texted me to let me know he purchased movie tickets. I've got forty-five minutes to get to the theater."

"Have a good time," Christian shouted out through the vehicle window to both his fellow instructors. "Don't do anything I wouldn't do."

"That would mean everything, since you don't have a girlfriend. Maybe you should correct that," Derik teased back through the window. "I'll see you at church on Sunday," he added before turning around and sauntering off.

Sometimes it was hard to be the only single instructor in his department. It wasn't that Christian hadn't tried dating; it was that every time he did, it never managed to work out. He'd tried all the usual ways: blind dates set-up by friends, joining the singles group at church, even the online dating apps didn't work for him. It was just easier focusing on his career, rather than continually putting himself out there and getting disappointed.

Christian parked the SUV and made his way to his apartment. After changing out of his uniform, he decided to go see if Jesse Dixon was free. Considering that the urban terrorist instructor was also single, and just as dedicated to his job as Christian was, he was fairly certain his friend wouldn't have plans tonight. Sure enough, only moments after Christian knocked on the other man's door, Jesse opened it.

"What's up, Christian?" he asked, leaning against the door frame. "Are you wanting to go to the gym before heading to the cafeteria for dinner?"

"Am I that predictable?" he asked, his cheeks turning red from embarrassment.

"Let's just say, you're a routine guy, which is fine. I am, too, probably from all my years in the bureau," Jesse said before taking a drink from his water bottle. Jesse was a former FBI agent who specialized in urban terrorism. He was recruited to Disaster City because of his expertise and excellent track-record at stopping domestic terrorism threats. "I've got my gym bag right here."

Jesse exited his apartment. They made their way to the neighboring building where the gym was housed in between the trainees' dormitories and the staff villa. The cafeteria and training center, with staff offices and classrooms, was across from there. With on-premises kennels, a medical clinic, and an auditorium, DCSRA was a full-fledged mini-city.

The men arrived at the nearly empty gym, ready for a hard workout. Christian liked that Jesse pushed him; he was an excellent workout partner.

"Where do you want to start? Squats? Presses?" Jesse asked, setting his bag down.

"My left shoulder has been stiff. I think we should start there."

Jesse nodded, heading over to the bench with the appropriate equipment, and Christian followed behind him. They were only a few minutes into their workout when Ben Miller, the assistant commander of the DCSRA, showed up in the gym. He made his way over to them.

"Glad I tracked you down, Perez. Sarge needs to see you in his office right away."

"What about?" Christian inquired, sitting up and swinging his legs over the side of the bench.

"I'll let him explain," Ben said, gesturing towards the exit. "Follow me."

Christian grabbed his towel and wrapped it around his neck, then stood up and grabbed his bag, swinging it over his shoulder. "I'll catch up with you later, Jesse."

"Sure thing, Christian," his friend said as he took his vacated spot on the workout bench.

"How long is this going to take? I'm supposed to pick up Cinder from the vet," Christian said, glancing at his watch.

"I'll call over and ask the doctor to stay until you can pick her up later," Ben offered.

"Thanks," Christian said as they entered the administrative section of the training center. The Commander's office was the largest in the building and set towards the back. They passed several closed doors before they reached the corner office.

Ben pushed the door open and moved inside, holding the door open for Christian so he could enter behind the senior instructor.

"Sorry to intrude on your time off, Perez, but this couldn't wait," the commander said as he looked up from his desk.

"Is something wrong? Did one of the trainees complain about my methods?" Christian asked defensively as he took a seat across from the middle-aged man with salt-and-peppered brown hair. He knew the material backwards and forwards, but he wasn't the most personable of instructors. It wouldn't be the first time that one of his students filed a grievance against him.

"No, nothing like that," his commander said with a shake of his head.

"Then what's going on?" Christian inquired with a puzzled look on his face. "Is there something else you need me to do; something for graduation tomorrow?"

Once again, Sarge's head shook from side-to-side. "I have a temporary assignment for you until the new recruits come in for the next class."

Christian stiffened, knowing that he wasn't going to like what was going to come out of his boss's mouth next.

"The fire chief from Dallas called and asked that we have our best arson investigator help with an ongoing case."

"Well, I don't know about best as much as the only one permanently on staff here at DCSRA," Christian said with a shrug.

"Please, Perez, modesty isn't a good color on you. We both know with all your extensive training and experience, you're the best arson investigator in the country. It's why the chief requested you by name. They've hit a dead end with their investigation and need Cinder's expert nose along with your knowledge."

Christian's brows came together in a furrow as he tried to come up with an excuse why he couldn't go. "I'm pretty busy getting ready for the next class…"

"This isn't a request, Perez. You're going to be taking care of this first thing Monday morning. One of the reasons that the DCSRA has been so successful is that we have the support from the locals around here, including the Dallas fire department. They don't often ask for our help, which means their backs must really be up against a wall. You're going to do this, and the quicker you get it done, the sooner you can get back here to get ready for the next class. Is that understood, Perez?"

Slowly, Christian nodded his head, realizing there was no point in arguing with Sarge. The man was as bull-headed as they came, and he always got what he wanted. Christian trudged out of the office, determined to get the new assignment done as quickly as possible so he could get back to his real job.

SNEAK PEAK OF LAWFULLY HEROIC

Adam Reynolds ran his hand through his brown hair with frustration. He wasn't sure how many more days he could take of his monotonous routine. He loved working with his K9 partner, Valor, but hated the endless row of cars they inspected daily at the Clear Mountain Army base.

"What's wrong? Are you dreaming of searching terrorists' strongholds for bombs again? You know you have to do years—not months—of posts like this before you ever get to do that," said Greg Walters, the other soldier assigned to the gate. "You should get used to this."

Adam knew Greg was right, but it didn't make him feel any better about the situation. The whole reason he renewed his contract was so that he could cross-train into a position as a K9 handler and go back overseas to detect IEDs. He wanted to stop the type of improvised bombs that killed his squad when he was stationed in Afghanistan. Working at the gate, he felt like he was spinning his wheels as much as the cars that continued to pass by.

A blue Honda Civic pulled up to the gate, and Greg checked the ID of the driver and passengers. Adam moved forward with Valor beside him, leading the German shepherd around the exterior of the car. He let his partner sniff every spot the expertly trained K9 deemed important. Once Valor came back to Adam's side signaling there was nothing to worry about, Adam waved the car through so it could enter the base. Same thing every time. Though he was glad there were no bombs coming onto the base, he wished he could be working an active hot zone.

"Want to go out with us after our shift?" Greg inquired while they waited for the next car to arrive. "We're heading over to The Lucky Penny to grab a couple of beers."

Adam averted his hazel eyes, knowing the other soldier wasn't going to like his answer. "Sorry, I can't; I have plans tonight."

"Let me guess, you have some sort of boring church thing again," Greg said with a roll of his eyes. "You seem to be going to those all the time."

"How about I go out with you guys next time?" Adam suggested, purposely avoiding talking about the activity the other soldier suspected. He didn't like the fact Greg made him feel bad about his plans. He also didn't want to get into a debate, or be forced to defend his choice to attend a men's hang-out started by some guys from Clear Mountain Assembly. It wasn't as stuffy as the other man made it sound. Sometimes they watched sporting events, other times they played cards, but mostly, it was just nice to have some friends that viewed life the same way he did. In the military, he never had that. All the guys ever wanted to do was chase girls and party at bars, neither of which really appealed to Adam.

"Sure, whatever, Adam, I'm not going to hold my breath. You always say you'll go out with us next time, but you never do."

The rest of the afternoon ambled by with more cars passing by without anything out of the ordinary. By the end, Adam was glad to be done with work and ready to have some fun with his friends.

Adam arrived at the rambling farmhouse on the

outskirts of town. He parked his truck, got Valor out of the passenger seat, and made his way up the steps. He knocked on the door, and a few minutes later, it swung open to reveal Officer Aiden O'Connell on the other side, one of the best K9 handlers he'd ever met. "Good to see you, Adam. Come on in. Everyone's waiting in the living room."

Adam made his way inside. The usual guys were there, including several of the Clear Mountain Police Search and Rescue team. Valor waited for Adam to give him the cue it was okay to take off and join Cooper and Harley, Aiden and Zach Turner's K9 partners. Once Adam released him from his leash, he took off running to the edge of the kitchen. He immediately started playing with one of the extra chew toys.

"Come take a seat. The game's about to start," Zach said, gesturing to a seat on the couch. "The pizza should be here in a few minutes."

Adam took the offered spot next to Liam Davis, a local business owner who ran a sleigh-ride company at Clear Mountain Resort. He was engaged to a Clear Mountain Police Detective and set to marry her in a few months.

"How was your day? As eventful as these two

who ended up using their K9 partners to track down a missing kid?" Liam asked with curiosity.

Adam shook his head. "No, just the same old, same old, for me. Valor and I spent our time checking out cars before they passed through the base gate."

"Hey, don't knock it. I would give anything to do what all of you do. I keep waiting for the Captain to add a third K9 position to the department, but he hasn't done it," said Ted Hendricks, another Clear Mountain Search and Rescue officer.

"Ted, your job is just as important as ours," Aiden corrected. "We're a team; don't ever forget that."

"I know that. I've just always wanted to be a K9 handler. Sometimes I think about applying to other departments, but now that I'm in a committed relationship with Deanna, I don't think I could leave her like that."

"Please don't," Zach jokingly begged with a wink. "We don't want our head dispatcher to end up mad because of it. She'd take it out on all of us."

"Okay everyone, the game's about to start," Connor Bishop, the head of the Clear Mountain SWAT team, said as he waved at all of them to be quiet. "I want to see the Broncos sweep the division."

The men settled in around the flat screen TV just as the kickoff took place. Adam enjoyed the rest of the evening with his friends, rooting for their native team and eating lots of junk food. He headed home knowing he was ready to fall fast asleep when his head hit the pillow. What he didn't expect was to find an invitation in his mailbox. It was offering Adam and Valor a chance to join the batch of new recruits for the training program at the elite Disaster City Search and Rescue Academy in Texas.

He'd sent in the application on a whim, never thinking that they would actually want him, let alone that his commanding officer would approve it. Despite the unlikelihood of it actually happening, he held it in his hands. It was physical proof that dreams really could come true. He knew he could finish this training at the top of his class. When he did just that, the Army would have to grant him a post of his choosing. This was the ticket he needed to get back overseas where he belonged.

Grab your copy of Lawfully Heroic!

SNEAK PEEK OF RESCUE AGENT FOR DANA

Right as the clock struck eight, Officer Joe Griffin, dressed in his freshly ironed blue cargo uniform, took his spot at the front of the Disaster City Search and Rescue Academy classroom. Fellow instructor, Ted Hendricks, went to the back and shut the door, making it clear that it was time to start the first session.

"Good morning, trainees," Joe began, as he had for the past six years while instructing new groups of K9 handlers each quarter. "Welcome to your first day at the most prestigious and elite urban and natural disaster search and rescue school in the world." The memorized speech rolled off his tongue like butter; he didn't even have to think about the words as he recited them. Instead, he paid close attention to the men and women sitting in front of him, sizing each of them up by the way they behaved. "Here, there is only one thing that matters. Our house, our rules. You will do things our way, which is the best and only way."

"DCSRA is the best of the best," Hendricks added, after Joe finished the first part of the welcome speech. "No matter how good you are, no matter what awards you've won, or how well you've performed at previous K9 trials, it means exactly zilch here at the academy. All of you have to prove to us that you belong here and deserve to receive the coveted DCSRA certificate of completion."

The other two instructors for their division, Officers Bilmont and Dixon, didn't miss a beat. They immediately started going over the expectations and requirements. The trainees whipped out their notepads and pens, furiously taking down notes so they wouldn't forget anything as the experienced instructors rattled off the massive list of information.

Out of habit, Joe walked the room with his German shepherd K9 partner, Legend, right beside him. Joe inspected the trainees, his gray eyes narrowing as he made a mental assessment about each of their work ethics based on the way they took notes. Even though Joe was doing exactly what he should, he could feel the restlessness stirring deep inside him again. Over the past year, the craving for change manifested in him regularly. He couldn't shake the feeling that it was time to do something else with his life.

Legend leaned against Joe's leg, clearly sensing the tension in him. His canine partner looked up at him with concern, causing Joe to be filled with frustration. *Get it together, Griffin. Focus on your job,* he chastised himself. *Stop letting your mind wander where it shouldn't.*

The instructors finished the rest of the morning lecture before releasing the class for lunch. In the afternoon, in order to allow the instructors to determine the capability of each recruit, the trainees would conduct their first practice search.

"What's going on with you, Griffin?" Dixon questioned from across the lunch table. "You seemed...distracted this morning."

"It's nothing," Joe stated, gesturing dismissively in the air. "I didn't sleep well last night, that's all."

"I'd wondered if it was first-day jitters, but you're too well-seasoned for that," Bilmont stated with a roll of his eyes. "I've never known a man more about the job than you, Griffin."

Joe purposely took a sip of his iced tea to avoid saying anything else. He knew what the other instructors thought of him, and the last thing he wanted to do was give them a reason to doubt his commitment to the job. When they weren't training handlers at the academy, they were out conducting search and rescues together assisting other agencies that needed help. It was important that his fellow teammates felt like they could rely on him and admitting to his recent apathy would only raise concerns.

"Leave him alone, Bilmont. We all know how Griffin is," Dixon stated with a shrug. "He's like a veteran bear that's made his permanent home in an old cave. For better or worse, we're stuck with him."

"Yes, but he's *our* grumpy bear," Bilmont said with a chuckle. "We'll never—"

Joe knew they were messing with him like they did on a regular basis. On any other day, it wouldn't have bothered him. Today, however, he couldn't help but feel the frustration about his current position seep out. Unable to tolerate their ribbing one moment longer, he jumped up from his chair, spun around, and took off without saying a word, Legend trailing behind him.

He had no idea where he was going. When he

ended up at the staff offices, he took it as a sign that he needed to go over a few details for the rest of the week. He turned on his computer and went through the agenda for the first week of the current class. He was nearly finished when he heard the familiar voices of his fellow instructors outside their office.

"You know, his reaction today probably has to do with what's happening at the end of this week," Bilmont told the other men.

"I know, every year this happens. I doubt he even realizes how much the anniversary affects him," Dixon added.

"What anniversary?" Hendricks asked in confusion. "Did you guys forget that I've barely been here a year? I don't know all of your guys' patterns yet."

"It's the anniversary of the 9/11 attacks. I can't even imagine being in New York when the planes hit the Towers, let alone at Ground Zero as they fell," Dixon explained. "He rarely talks about it, and never in detail, but it's clear what happened during the attack did a number on him."

"It only makes sense that he isn't sleeping well. I bet he has all sorts of nightmares from that day and the search and recovery he did afterward," Hendricks stated with clear pity in his voice. "I wouldn't wish that job on any officer. Do you think we should ask him how's he doing with the anniversary coming up?"

"No," both Bilmont and Dixon blurted out in unison.

"If he wants to talk about it, he'll bring it up," Dixon added. "But Griffin plays most everything pretty close to the vest."

Joe didn't like the other instructors discussing his past. It meant that he hadn't been doing a good job of keeping his feelings under control, and that wasn't like him. If he was honest with himself, the upcoming anniversary had been bothering him more than usual. He'd always managed to push away the pain from that day, but lately, Melanie's memory had been popping up when he least expected it. Part of him wondered if it had to do with the girl he rescued last month during a flood in Northwest Texas. She looked a lot like Melanie, from her red hair, to her sprinkle of freckles across the bridge of her nose. He was glad he was able to save the girl, but it brought back the pain of failing Melanie. If he had just been able to get to her in the Towers, maybe his whole life would be different now. Instead, he was forced to live with the knowledge that the biggest failure of his career took away the most important person in his life.

He stood up from his desk and marched across the office, yanking open the door and startling the other three men in the process. All of their heads jerked toward him, eyes wide with shock.

"We didn't know you were in there," Hendricks stammered out, his cheeks tinged red with embarrassment.

"I was just leaving. It's time to head back to the classroom." Joe firmly shut the door and pushed through the group. "Come on, we don't have all day," he added over his shoulder.

The trainees didn't get very far into the practice course before Ben Miller, the salt-and-pepper haired deputy commander of the academy, showed up with an emergency assignment for them. "There was a massive flood in northern New Mexico that caused several mudslides. They need help searching for survivors and asked us to send over any available officers. I know you just started training this group, so they can't go since we aren't sure how they will do. I'll take over the class with Sarge while the four of you head to New Mexico. The helicopter is already on standby, so gear up and get out of here."

Joe, along with the rest of his team, made quick work of getting ready. Once they gathered all the necessary search and rescue equipment, they placed their K9 partners inside the kennels on the chopper and took off for their mission.

Joe tried to focus on getting his head straight for the grueling hours of search and rescue that lay ahead, but his mind kept drifting back to what he overheard the rest of his team discussing. Between his time at the academy and his twenty years with the New York City Police Department, his search and rescue tenure was extensive. He'd managed for years to keep the stress under control, but he wondered if constantly seeing desperate people in disastrous scenarios had finally caught up to him. It wasn't easy to handle and often took a harsh toll on an officer. Was his time in the field finally up? What did that mean for him? Joe's whole life revolved around search and rescue. If he retired now, he wasn't even sure who he would be without it. He'd chosen to focus on his career rather than take the time to start a family, leaving him squarely as a confirmed bachelor with his K9 partner, Legend, as his only child, and his fellow instructors as his family. What would his life look like if he left that world behind him?

"We're here," Dixon announced as the helicopter landed on a clear patch of dirt near the command center for the search and rescue operation. "Let's get to it."

The team hopped out of the helicopter and quickly got their instructions. They were assigned to assist in searching several camping areas in the Carson National Forest. After hitching a ride with some of the U.S. Forest Service Rangers to the location, they placed their rescue pack on their backs and made sure their K9 partners' vests were secure before giving the command for them to search the first area.

Joe sent up a silent prayer, asking God to guide their steps as they conducted their search. They methodically worked their way through the disheveled terrain littered with chunks of mud, rocks, and broken pieces of trees. There was a piece of a roof poking out from a large deposit of mud. "That could be something," Hendricks stated, as he pointed to the mostly obscured area. "It could be part of the campground. We should go check it out."

"Good catch," Dixon praised as they made their way over. "If the campers had any warning, they might have tried to go into the structure to hide."

The foursome made their way over to the new section and set their dogs to the task of investigating. At first, nothing seemed out of the ordinary, but as they moved from the edges of the area further in, the faint sound of muffled cries penetrated the air.

"Do you hear that?" Joe asked the group. "I think there's someone in there."

The team placed their bags down on the ground and pulled out their collapsible shovels. They gently scooped up mud, being careful to cause as little disturbance as possible so the debris wouldn't fall into the structure and cause more damage. Once they reached about midway down, a window became visible. The glass was gone, pushed in from the mud.

"That's our way inside," Hendricks declared with optimism, as the sounds of the crying grew louder.

Dixon and his K9 partner were the first ones through the window, followed by Hendricks and Joe who brought up the rear. Bilmont remained outside to keep an eye on the surrounding area, and to assist with helping any possible victims out of the structure.

Inside, they turned on their flashlights and scanned the area, which turned out to be a restroom facility. As they moved further into the structure, they looked for the source of the cries. In the far corner of the building, there was a small boy, who looked to be about seven years old. He was huddled in the corner, next to an unconscious man.

"Hello, I'm Officer Hendricks and I'm here to help you," Joe's colleague said as he approached the boy. "Are you hurt?"

The young boy shook his head. "I'm okay, but my dad's not. When the ground started to shift, he rushed me in here. He hit his head when he tried to close the door and got a bad headache and couldn't stay awake."

Joe bent down and inspected the boy's father. There was a large bump as well as a cut above his right brow. He bandaged it up, then quickly inspected the victim for any other injuries. When he didn't see any, he assessed he was suffering from a concussion. Just to be safe; however, Joe placed a protective collar around the other man's neck. He gently tapped his arm to see if he could wake him up. "Sir, can you hear me? I'm Officer Griffin with Disaster City Search and Rescue. You were caught in a mudslide, but we're here to help."

The man's eyelids fluttered for a couple of seconds, as if processing what Joe just said. He opened his mouth and stammered out, "How's my son?"

"I'm fine, Dad, I'm right here." The young boy patted his father's arm.

"We're going to get you both out of here," Dixon, who was beside Joe, stated. "And we need to do it right away. We don't want to take the chance that another shift of the ground above could cause this place to cave in on itself."

"Can you both walk?" Joe inquired.

Both victims nodded, prompting Hendricks to help the boy to the window first. Joe and Dixon assisted the father into a standing position. Both officers followed after them to assure he remained mobile. Bilmont retrieved the boy and had him move out of the way. Dixon went through next to assist with pulling the father out from the other side.

Joe helped the man through the window. On the other side, Bilmont and Dixon secured him just as the ground started to shift again.

"Get out of there," Dixon shouted to Hendricks and Joe.

"You go first," Joe ordered Hendricks, knowing his friend had a pregnant wife waiting for him at home. "I'm right behind you."

Once the junior search and rescue officer was through the window, Joe scurried out after him. He made it out just in time, because a few moments later, a fresh section of mud slid down the nearby hill, covering the top of the structure just as the group rushed out of the way.

Dixon called in the helicopter to evacuate the victims. While they waited, they gave them snacks and drinks.

"Thank you for helping us," the father stated as they climbed onto the chopper. "We owe you our lives."

"It was nothing," Dixon stated with a warm smile. "We were glad to help."

"It was everything," the man countered, waving goodbye. "And I'll never forget it."

They gave their K9 partners water in travel bowls while they drank from their own water bottles. Even though they all wanted to keep going, it was important to take a small break and hydrate.

"That was a close one," Hendricks stated with a sigh. "Promise me, you won't tell Deanna about this one."

"You can bet I won't. I'm not going to incite the anger of a pregnant woman," Bilmont stated as he took a swig from his bottle.

"We should get back at it," Joe stated as he stood up from one of the boulders they were sitting on. "There could be more victims out here waiting for us to find them."

The team continued to search the campgrounds but didn't turn up any new victims. They were about to head back to command for a new assignment, when in the distance, Joe noticed a group of people on horseback. Confused, he almost thought he was seeing things from his lack of sleep the past couple of nights. It was only when he heard Bilmont shout with surprise, "Cowboys out here in the middle of a disaster area. Now I've seen it all," Joe knew it wasn't a mirage.

"What do you think they are doing out here?" Hendricks asked with curiosity.

"I have no idea," Joe mumbled under his breath as he ran his hand through his dark hair, his own curiosity growing by the minute.

Since moving to Texas six years prior, Joe had adopted the cowboy lifestyle, donning the hat and wranglers on his days off, as well as learning how to ride horses in his free time. He'd even mulled over the idea of buying a ranch near the academy, but decided against it, knowing with his job, he didn't have time to take care of it.

"You should flag them down and talk to them,

Griffin. You probably speak the same language," Dixon teased.

"I bet they're fluent in bullheaded bronco," Bilmont added with a chuckle.

The other instructors were relentless about razzing Joe about how odd it was to have a born-and-bred New Yorker morph into a Texan cowboy. He couldn't help that he was drawn to the lifestyle, despite it being a strong contrast to how he grew up.

Before Joe knew what was happening, Hendricks was doing exactly what the other two officers suggested. He was waving at the cowboys, saying, "Hey, over here."

The two men came trotting up on their set of brown horses. As they got closer, Joe noticed that though they were wearing Wranglers and Stetson's, they also had shiny gold badges on the right side of their flannel shirts. *Wild Animal Protection Agency* was scrolled across the emblem. Joe had never heard of the agency and wondered what they did.

"Are you guys out here searching for victims?" one of the cowboys asked, scanning them up and down. "We heard there might be some trapped victims at the nearby campgrounds."

"We already searched the area and found a

father and son," Joe stated, his need to defend his team manifesting out of nowhere. Why did he feel like he had to prove himself to these men? He didn't even know them, but somehow, he felt like it was important they respected him.

"I'm Rescue Agent Brian Crawford, and my partner here is Senior Rescue Agent Richard Dooley. We're with the Wild Animal Protection Agency," the dark-haired, younger cowboy stated as an introduction.

"What are you doing out here?" Joe asked, unable to help himself from prying into their reason for being in such a remote area during a disaster.

The second blond-haired man, who looked to be a few years older than the other agent, gave their reason for being there. "We're looking for a lost herd of wild mustang. The Bureau of Land Management requested us to come out and secure the herd that was last known to be inside this mudslide area. They were supposed to remain in the Jicarilla Wild Horse Territory but had wandered out of the area just before the flood hit and caused the slide."

"Is there anything we can do to help?" Joe offered, surprising even himself by doing it.

"Thanks for the offer, but herding the mustangs

requires us to work from horseback," the first agent explained. "We'll let you get back to your own mission."

The two groups took off in separate directions, but Joe found himself trailing behind the rest of his team, constantly looking over his shoulder at the cowboys disappearing out of sight. Their job intrigued him, making him wonder what it would be like to work at an agency like that.

Legend must have sensed something, because he started to bark, then moved towards a hilly area to the west of them. "What is it, boy?" Joe asked, following behind him. "Is there a victim this way?"

"What's going on, Griffin?" Dixon asked from the front of the group. "Did Legend find something?"

"I don't think so," Joe hollered back. "I think it's most likely a small animal, but just to be sure, we'll go check it out. You guys keep going, and I'll radio you to come back if it's a victim."

Joe moved along the bottom of the hill, keeping his eyes peeled for any sign of movement as he followed Legend. There was a stirring behind a large thicket of bushes, confirming Joe's theory that it was most likely an animal rather than a person.

"Did you hear a groundhog, Legend?"

When he barked again, there was a sound that immediately made Joe realize it wasn't a rodent at all. The neighing sound belonged to a young foal that didn't look to be any older than six months. The animal was tangled up in the brush with her hooves trapped in the mud.

"Whoa, there, girl," Joe said, moving towards the horse in a slow and steady pace. The foal was skittish, clearly unfamiliar with people, but had no way of escaping. Joe was certain if the young horse could run off, it would. "It's all right; I can help you."

Joe pulled out his shovel and carefully dug around the horse's legs. Once all four were free, the foal backed away, but there was a rock wall behind her. She neighed in fear, but Joe didn't let it keep him from trying to help her. He slowly reached out and placed his hand on the bridge of her nose. "Easy, girl, easy."

The young horse must have sensed his good intentions because she calmed down and let him guide her out of the thicket. As soon as she was free; however, she took off, heading towards the worst part of the mudslide.

"Legend, cut her off," Joe shouted with trepidation, knowing there was no way he was fast enough to do the job. His K9 partner did what Joe commanded, chasing after the foal. He barked, then circled the horse, causing her to stop in her tracks.

"This way, Legend, bring her this way towards me," Joe ordered, knowing she was safer heading in the direction of the rescue agents that just left.

Legend barked repeatedly as he paced back and forth in front of the horse, causing her to turn around and run the opposite way, just as Joe wanted.

They ran after her, Legend keeping a pretty good pace but making sure to move in front of her when needed to keep her from getting too far ahead of them. Before he knew it, they were catching up to the rescue agents.

They stopped and turned around, surprised to not only see them but also the young horse with them.

"What's going on here?" Rescue Agent Dooley questioned, glancing between the two animals and Joe.

"We found this foal and thought we would bring her to you," Joe explained, realizing it might seem silly when he could have just called in the location, he added, "I hope we didn't overstep."

"No, I'm just surprised you were able to do it,"

Dooley admitted. "Wild horses are difficult to herd, especially on foot. It must mean you and your K9 partner are naturals. Maybe you're in the wrong profession."

"He's right," Rescue Agent Crawford agreed, pulling out a card from his shirt pocket and handing it to Joe. "If you ever think about switching agencies, you could be a real asset to WAPA. We could use a search and rescue team like the two of you."

Grab your copy of Rescue Agent for Dana.

A NOTE FROM THE AUTHOR

I hope you have enjoyed *The Girlfriend Rescue* and plan to read the rest of Disaster City Search and Rescue as well as of the books in my other K-9 series, The Lawkeepers. You can also read the prequel, Adam's story, Lawfully Heroic, part of the Lawkeeper series to find out more about Disaster City and the people who work there. Lastly, I have a spin-off series from DCSR, the Wild Animal Protection Agency so you can check that out as well.

Your opinion and support matters, so I would greatly appreciate you taking the time to leave a review. If you would like more info, please join my Newsletter and get a free novella just for signing up. I'd_also love for you to check out My Reader's Group!

Jenna Brandt

ALSO BY JENNA BRANDT

Most Books are Free in Kindle Unlimited too!

Disaster City Search and Rescue

Step into the world of Disaster City Search and Rescue, where officers, firefighters, military, and medics, train and work alongside each other with the dogs they love, to do the most dangerous job of all — help lost and injured victims find their way home.

The Girlfriend Rescue

The Billionaire Rescue

The Movie Star Rescue

The Best Friend Rescue

The Ex-Wife Rescue

The Cowgirl Rescue

The Single Mom Rescue

The Pop Singer Rescue

Wild Animal Protection Agency

Come be apart of the adventure, danger, and heartfelt moments with the Wild Animal Protection Agency, where brave men and women work alongside each other all over the world, to do the most risky job of all — rescue injured and endangered wild animals.

Rescue Agent for Dana

Rescue Agent for Sarah

Rescue Agent for Kylie

Rescue Agent for Josette

Rescue Agent for Margo

Rescue Agent for Penny

Billionaires of Manhattan Series

The billionaires that live in Manhattan and the women who love them. If you love epic dates, grand romantic gestures, and men in suits with hearts of gold, then these are books are perfect for you.

Waiting on the Billionaire

Nanny for the Billionaire

Merging with the Billionaire

(**Entire series on Audiobook**)

Second Chance Islands

What's better than billionaires on islands? How about billionaires finding second chances at life, love, and redemption while on one.

The Billionaire's Repeat

(Free the you join my newsletter)

The Billionaire's Reunion

The Billionaire's Hideaway

The Billionaire's Duty

The Billionaire's Christmas

Billionaire Birthday Club

An exclusive resort—for the billionaire who appears to have everything but secretly wants more. After filling out a confidential survey, a curated celebration is waiting on the island to make their birthday wishes come true!

The Billionaire's Birthday Wish

The Billionaire's Birthday Surprise

The Billionaire's Birthday Gift

The Lawkeepers

A multi-author series alternating between historical westerns and contemporary westerns featuring law enforcement heroes that span multiple agencies and generations. Join bestselling author Jenna Brandt and many others as they weave captivating, sweet and inspirational stories of romance and suspense between the lawkeepers — and the women who love them. The

Lawkeepers is a world like no other; a world where lawkeepers and heroes are honored with unforgettable stories, characters, and love.

Jenna's Lawkeeper books:

Contemporary

Lawfully Adored-K-9

Lawfully Wedded-K-9

Lawfully Treasured-SWAT

Lawfully Dashing-Female Cop/Christmas

Lawfully Devoted-Billionaire Bodyguard/K-9

Lawfully Heroic-Military Police

Lawfully Contemporary Box Set

Historical

Lawfully Loved-Texas Sheriff

Lawfully Wanted-Bounty Hunter

Lawfully Forgiven-Texas Ranger

Lawfully Avenged-US Marshal

Lawfully Covert-Spies

Lawfully Historical Box Set

Mail Order Mix-Up Series

Mail order bride books about women venturing out West to make new lives for themselves. What happens when they decide to take a chance on love along the way?

Mail Order Misfit

Mail Order Misstep

Mail Order Miscast

Mail Order Misaim

Mail Order Misplay

Mail Order Mister

Mail Order Mishap

Widows, Brides, and Secret Babies

Mail order bride stories with a twist. What happens when a bride arrives pregnant or with a secret child?

Mail Order Miranda

Mail Order Miriam

Secret Baby Dilemma

Each mail order bride arrives with a baby or pregnant, and the prospective groom doesn't know until her arrival.

Mail Order Madeline

The Civil War Brides Trilogy

During the bloodiest conflict on American soil, two families struggle in the South to not only survive but to thrive.

Saved by Faith

Freed by Hope

Healed by Grace

Border Brides Series

Centered around the Old West border towns and the brides who end up there looking for a new start.

Discreetly Matched

June's Remedy

Becca's Lost Love

Hard to Please

The Window to the Heart Saga

A recountal of the epic journey of Lady Margaret, a young English noblewoman, who through many trials, obstacles, and tragedies, discovers her own inner strength, the sustaining force of faith in God, and the power of family and friends. In this three-part series, experience new places and cultures as the heroine travels from England to France and completes her adventures in America. The series has compelling themes of love, loss, faith and hope with an exceptionally gratifying conclusion.

Trilogy

The English Proposal (Book 1)

The French Encounter (Book 2)

The American Conquest (Book 3)

Spin-offs

The Oregon Pursuit (Book 1)

The White Weddings (Book 2)

The Viscount's Wife (Book 3)

The Window to the Heart Saga

Trilogy Box Set

The Window to the Heart Saga

Spin-off Books Box Set

The Window to the Heart Saga

Complete Collection Box Set

For more information about Jenna Brandt, signup for her Newsletter or visit her on any of her social media platforms:

www.JennaBrandt.com

www.facebook.com/JennaBrandtAuthor

Jenna Brandt's Reader Group

www.twitter.com/JennaDBrandt

www.instagram.com/jennabrandtauthor

JOIN MY MAILING LIST AND READER'S GROUPS

Sign-up for my newsletter and get a FREE book and a FREE short story.

Join my Reader's Group, Jenna's Joyful Page Turners, and get access to exclusive content and contests.

Join my multi-author reader's group, Heroes and Hunks, for fun with some of your favorite sweet authors

ACKNOWLEDGMENTS

My writing journey would not be possible without those who supported me. Since I can remember, writing is the only thing I love to do, and my deepest desire is to share my talent with others.

First and foremost, I am eternally grateful to Jesus, my lord and savior, who created me with this "writing bug" DNA.

In addition, many thanks go to:

My husband, Dustin, and three daughters, Katie, Julie, and Nikki, for loving me and supporting me during all my late-night writing marathons and coffee-infused mornings.

My mother, Connie, for being my first and most honest critic, now and always. As a little girl, sleeping under your desk during late-night deadlines for the local paper showed me what being a dedicated writer looked like.

My angels in heaven: my grandmother, who passed away in 2001; my infant son, Dylan, who was taken by SIDS seven years ago; and my father, who left us six years ago.

To Ginny Sterling and Jo Grafford, my best writing buddies, my comrades-in-arms, my sounding boards, my voices of reason, my partners in all things author. I love you ladies so much.

To my ARC Angels and Beta Bells for taking the time to read my story and give valuable feedback.

And lastly, but so important, to my dedicated readers, who have shared their love of my books with others, helping to spread the words about my stories. Your devotion means a great deal.

ABOUT THE AUTHOR

Jenna Brandt is an international bestselling and award-winning author who writes historical and contemporary romance. Her historical books span from Victorian to Western eras and all of her books have elements of romance, suspense and faith. She has her own best-selling historical series, Window to the Heart Saga, Mail Order Mix-Up, and Civil War Brides, as well as contemporary series, Billionaires of Manhattan, Second Chance Islands and the Wild Animal Protection Agency. Additionally, she's created two best-selling multi-author series, The Lawkeepers and Disaster City Search and Rescue based off the life of her husband in law enforcement. Both of her books, Waiting on the Billionaire and Lawfully Treasured, were voted into the Top 50 Indie Books of 2018 on Readfreely.com.

She's been an avid reader since she could hold a book and started writing stories almost as early. She's been published in several newspapers as well as edited for multiple papers, and graduated with her Bachelor of Arts degree in English from Bethany College where she was the Editor-in-Chief of the newspaper. Her first blog was published on The Mighty website, Yahoo Parenting and The Grief Toolbox as well as featured on the ABC News, CNN Health, and Good Morning America websites. She's also a member of the American Christian Fiction Writers (ACFW) association.

Writing is her passion, but she also enjoys date nights with her hubby, cooking from scratch, watching movies on Netflix, reading books by her author friends, and engaging in social media with her readers. Her three young daughters keep her busy with Girl Scout activities, going to the mall, and playing at the park where they live in the Central Valley of California. She summers on the Golden Central Coast where she finds endless inspiration for her romance books. She's also active in her local church where she volunteers on their first impressions team.

CPSIA information can be obtained
at www.ICGtesting.com
Printed in the USA
LVHW090706060921
697066LV00009BA/48